stuck inside!

EERIE, INDIANA
1917

#5 HAVE YOURSELF
AN EERIE LITTLE CHRISTMAS

#5 HAVE YOURSELF
AN EERIE LITTLE CHRISTMAS

MIKE FORD

AN AVON CAMELOT BOOK

AVON BOOKS
A division of
The Hearst Corporation
1350 Avenue of the Americas
New York, New York 10019

First Avon Camelot Printing: December 1997

CAMELOT TRADEMARK REG. U.S. PAT. OFF. AND IN OTHER COUNTRIES, MARCA REGISTRADA, HECHO EN U.S.A.

Printed in the U.S.A.

OPM 10 9 8 7 6 5 4 3 2 1

PROLOGUE

PROLOGUE

*M*y name is Marshall Teller. Not too long ago, I was living in New Jersey, just across the river from New York City. It was crowded, polluted, and full of crime. I loved it. But my parents wanted a better life for my sister and me. So we moved to a place so wholesome, so squeaky clean, so ordinary that you could only find it on TV—Eerie, Indiana.

It's the American Dream come true, right? Wrong. Sure, my new hometown *looks* normal enough. But look again. Underneath, it's crawling with strange stuff. Item: Elvis lives on my paper route. Item: Bigfoot eats out of my trash. Item: I see unexplained flashing lights in the sky at least once a week. No one believes me, but Eerie is the center of weirdness for the entire planet.

Since I moved here, I've been attacked by a werewolf, had my brain sucked out and put back in, delivered a letter for a ghost, and been stalked by a grudge-bearing tornado named Bob. Every time something strange happens, I think my life can't get any more peculiar. But then I turn a corner and there's something even stranger waiting for me. But no matter how weird Eerie gets, nobody else seems to notice.

Nobody except my friend Simon Holmes. Simon's my next-door neighbor. He's lived in Eerie his whole life, and he's the only other person who knows just how freaky this place is. Together, we've been keeping a record of all the stuff that happens around here. We've faced some of Eerie's most bizarre inhabitants and lived to tell about it, from the talking dogs that tried to take over the city to the crazy woman who kidnapped us and tried to keep us locked up forever in giant plastic kitchenware. I told you this place was weird.

Still don't believe me? You will.

1

When Simon and I walked into World of Stuff, the place was packed with people. It was two days before Christmas, and from the look of things, everyone in Eerie had put off their gift buying until the last minute. It was all we could do to push our way through the mass of bodies that crowded the store as people ran around snatching items off of shelves and rummaging through boxes to find the perfect presents.

"Excuse me," I said as I bumped into someone.

"No, excuse us," said two voices together. It was the Wilson twins—Bert and Ernie. They were leaving the store with their arms loaded up with bags. They had on matching red hats and red scarves.

"Merry Christmas," they said in unison.

"Same to you," I said.

To tell the truth, I wasn't exactly in the Christmas spirit. There it was just a few days away, and I hadn't even started to get excited about it. I don't really know why. Maybe it was because I was getting older, and some of the magic I'd felt about the holiday when I was a kid was gone. Or maybe it was because it hadn't even snowed once yet. I'd been hoping for a white Christmas, but so far the streets of Eerie were bare. Not even the giant twinkling candy canes strung all along Main Street made me feel jolly.

Whatever the reason, I just couldn't seem to get enthused about the whole holiday thing. That's why I'd waited until almost the last day before buying presents for my family. All day I'd been dragging Simon around the mall looking for stuff. I'd managed to find things for my father (a book on the history of corn) and Syndi (a cool new scrapbook for her collection of articles on people who disappeared), but there wasn't anything at the mall I thought my mother might like. I needed something special for her.

Finally, I'd given up and decided to try World of Stuff. Mr. Radford has the biggest collection of unique things in all of Eerie. If I couldn't find something there, I would just have to resort to that old standby gift: gloves. I didn't want to do that.

"Geez, it looks like everyone in town had the same idea you did, Mars," said Simon. "There won't be anything left by the time they're done."

I sighed. "Well, let's just look," I said. "There has to be *something* here I can give my mom."

We pushed our way to the back of the store, barely avoiding getting run over by Mayor Chisel as he raced by with a giant globe held over his head. "Just what I've always wanted!" he said as he went by. "The whole world! Just for me."

The back of the store was a little less crowded, probably because that's where Mr. Radford keeps the older things he finds at rummage sales and auctions. It's actually my favorite part of the store. Once I found a Babe Ruth baseball card stuck inside a book I picked out of a box back there.

"What kind of thing are you looking for?" asked Simon as we examined the shelves.

"I'm not sure," I said. "But I'll know it when I see it. What did you get your mom?"

"A basketball," said Simon.

"A basketball?" I said.

Simon shrugged. "It's what she asked for," he said. "When she sprained her ankle a few months ago she spent all her time in bed watching basketball on TV. Now she thinks she wants to be a basketball player. Don't ask. Last year she was determined to be a hockey goalie. She lost a tooth at her first practice."

There were certainly a lot of interesting things in World of Stuff, but I was having trouble finding just the right gift for my mom. Even though I thought they were cool, I knew she wouldn't be thrilled with a goldfish bowl shaped like a cat's head, salt and pepper shakers that looked like dancing cows, or a painting of dogs playing cards.

"This is hopeless," I said. "I might as well just buy the gloves and get it over with."

"Wait a minute," said Simon. "Let's see what's in this box."

He'd found an old cardboard box sitting in the corner. It was totally covered in dust, and it looked as though it hadn't been opened in about a hundred years.

"It's probably just junk," I said, but I knelt down and watched as he opened the top. Inside, the box was filled with lots of old newspaper wadded up into balls.

"See?" I said. "Nothing."

But Simon started looking through the box anyway. He picked up one of the newspaper balls and held it in his hand.

"It's sort of heavy," he said. "There must be something inside."

Carefully unwrapping the paper, he revealed a shiny blue ball. There was a string attached to one end.

"See?" he said. "It's a Christmas ornament. And it looks like a really old one. I bet it's made out of glass."

I picked up another paper ball and unwrapped it. Inside was another ornament, this one shaped like a strawberry and covered in a dusting of white sparkles.

"These are pretty neat," I said. "But I don't think my mom would flip over them."

"Yeah, but I bet she'd think *this* is really great," said Simon.

He had unwrapped another package. Only this one

wasn't an ornament. It was a large glass globe filled with water. And inside the globe there was a miniature model of a city.

"What is that?" I said.

"It's a snow globe," said Simon. "Haven't you ever seen one?"

I shook my head.

"Watch." He turned the globe over and shook it gently. When he turned it right side up again, the water was filled with little flakes of swirling whiteness. The miniature town was surrounded by what looked like a blinding snowstorm.

"That's amazing," I said. "I know my mom would really like that. It's just like the kind of pretty, useless thing she's always bringing home from antique stores and yard sales."

We put the ornaments back into the box and sealed it up again. Then I rewrapped the snow globe and carried it to the front of the store, narrowly escaping getting knocked over by the King and his friend Marilyn as they rushed in.

"Excuse me, little paper boy," said the King from behind his big sunglasses.

"Ooh," added Marilyn in her squeaky voice. "Have a merry Christmas, boys."

I put the snow globe on the counter and nodded at Mr. Radford as he rang it up on the cash register.

"Sure is busy today," said Mr. Radford as he put the globe into a bag.

"Everyone's doing their last-minute Christmas shopping," said Simon.

Mr. Radford snapped his fingers. "Aha. So that's why it's so crowded," he said. "I knew something must be going on. It's Christmas. Thank you for pointing it out. Next year I'll know."

I looked at Simon. I couldn't believe Mr. Radford would forget something as big as Christmas. Then again, this is Eerie, where anything can happen. I decided it was better not to say anything else.

I handed Mr. Radford my money and he gave me my change. I took the package from him, and Simon and I left. Outside, there were people walking up and down Main Street underneath the twinkling red and white lights of the electric candy canes.

"Am I glad to have all my shopping done," I said.

"Now all you have to do is wrap everything," said Simon.

"I'll do that tonight," I said. "You want to come over?"

"Sure," said Simon. "My parents are going to a Christmas party tonight anyway. Hey, I'll bring the tape of that movie I told you about, *Alien Christmas.* It's about this UFO that invades the world disguised as Santa's sleigh. Everyone thinks they're getting presents, but

8

the boxes are all filled with mutant creatures from Pluto.''

''Sounds really festive,'' I joked. ''I'm sure it's just the thing to put me in the holiday mood.''

When I got home, my mother was in the kitchen. Smoke was pouring out of the oven, and she was frantically trying to wave it out the open window.

''What happened?'' I said, grabbing a dish towel and fanning the smoke out the back door.

''I was trying to make gingerbread boys,'' she said, pointing to a cookie sheet sitting on the counter. On the tray were some misshapen figures that had been burned to a crisp.

''I guess I shouldn't have tried dressing them in little paper outfits before I baked them,'' my mother said. ''It's just that they looked so cute.''

Baking is not my mother's greatest achievement. But every year at Christmas she tries to make something, and it always ends up being a disaster. ''That's okay, mom,'' I said. ''None of us really likes gingerbread anyway. Just stick to the eggnog. At least that comes in a carton.''

My mother frowned. ''It's just that I wanted this Christmas to be different,'' she said.

I put my arm around her. ''Sometimes it's nice to be plain old normal,'' I said, thinking about everything I'd seen in Eerie over the past year. "Let's try for a nice ordinary Christmas."

I left her in the kitchen, still trying to clear out the smoke, and went up to my room. I put the bag from World of Stuff in my closet with the other presents. For the rest of the afternoon, I caught up on my favorite comics.

As planned, Simon came by after dinner. I got the presents from my closet, along with some wrapping paper and tape, and we took it all up to the Secret Spot. Everyone knows to leave us alone when we're up there, so I knew we wouldn't be disturbed. While Simon played around with the telescope we keep up there, scanning the December sky for signs of anything weird, I wrapped presents.

My dad's book was easy to wrap. So was Syndi's scrapbook. But I wasn't sure how to wrap something round like the snow globe. I picked it up and held it in my hand, turning it around and around as I tried to think of a cool way to wrap it up.

As I turned it, I stared at the little town trapped inside the curved glass walls of the globe. The detail was really amazing. Whoever had made the snow globe had taken great care to make sure the buildings of the town and even the little people walking through its streets looked as real as possible. I couldn't help but stare at the windows of the houses, from behind which light seemed to stream out as though there were people inside eating dinner. I could even see the faces of the people as they bustled about the little streets, carrying packages in their arms.

One house in particular caught my attention. It was a large house on the edge of town. It had big windows that looked out onto the street. Standing in one of the windows was a young woman. There was a group of people standing on the street who looked like they were singing Christmas carols. The young woman in the house was watching them, but instead of looking happy, she looked very sad. As I stared at her face, I wondered why whoever made the globe had put her into it.

I turned the globe over and shook it gently. When I turned it back again, the town flurried with snow. It landed on the shoulders of the carolers and on the roof of the house with the big windows. It made a soft screen of white across everything.

"I wish it would snow," I said. "I wish it would snow just like that."

"What?" said Simon. "Did you say something?"

"I was just thinking how great it would be if it snowed," I said.

"I can't ever remember there being snow at Christmas in Eerie," said Simon. "Isn't that weird?"

"What?" I said. "Something weird in *Eerie*? You must have this mixed up with some other town. *Nothing* weird ever happens here."

Simon laughed. "If you're not going to wrap that, let's watch the movie."

He took *Alien Christmas* and put the tape into the VCR, and we settled down to enjoy the movie. Simon was going to stay over, so we'd set up sleeping bags on the floor and brought up a bunch of snacks. As the opening credits of the film rolled, I opened a bag of chips and started eating. After a few minutes, I forgot all about the snow globe and the wish I'd made.

The movie was as good as Simon had said it was. The special effects were amazing, and for once I actually didn't figure out the ending before it happened. When the hero's dog turned out to be one of the aliens, I was really surprised.

"That was perfect," I told Simon when it was over. "We'll have to watch it again tomorrow."

I yawned and looked at the clock. It was just about midnight. I turned out the light and we got into our sleeping bags. As I fell asleep, I looked at the snow globe sitting on my desk. The moonlight coming in the window was shining on it, and I could see that inside the glass sphere the snow was still swirling and blowing. The whole town was engulfed in a snowstorm.

"I must have shaken it harder than I thought I did," I thought to myself as I drifted off to sleep.

The next morning, I was awakened by Simon shaking my shoulder.

"Wake up!" he said excitedly. "You've got to see this."

"What?" I said sleepily. I sat up, rubbing my eyes.

Simon pointed to the window, but I couldn't see anything unusual.

"The sky is all white," I said. "So what?"

"It's not the sky," said Simon. "It's snow! There's a huge blizzard going on. The whole town is buried."

For some reason, I looked immediately at the snow globe on my desk. Inside its glass walls, the snowstorm was still raging, as though it had never stopped.

2

"Did you touch that?" I asked Simon, nodding toward the snow globe.

"No," he said. "Why?"

"The last time I shook that thing was last night," I said. "And it's still snowing. That's just not possible."

I got out of the sleeping bag and went to the window. Outside, everything was covered in a thick blanket of snow. The trees were all wearing fluffy coats of white, and the cars in the streets had been turned into small mounds. A few people had ventured outside, and they were standing around looking at the winter wonderland that had sprung up overnight.

"How did it snow this much in one night?" said Simon. "There wasn't even a flurry when we went to bed, and that was almost midnight."

I went to my desk and picked up the snow globe. I turned it upside down and waited for all the snow to tumble to the bottom. But it just kept swirling around and around in the glass bubble, as though it were no longer just water and bits of fake snow, but something else. Something with a mind of its own. Something alive.

No matter which way I turned the snow globe or how much I shook it, the blizzard continued to blow, just like the one that had wrapped itself around Eerie.

"What are you thinking?" asked Simon, watching me shake the globe.

"I'm not sure," I said. "All I know is that last night I shook this and wished it would snow, and now this morning it really *is* snowing."

"So now you think that thing is magic or something?" said Simon. "This is just a snowstorm. A big one, that's for sure, but just a snowstorm. And just in time for Christmas. You should be happy. It's what you wanted."

"Maybe," I said. But inside I knew it was more than that. I wasn't sure how the real blizzard was connected to the one inside the snow globe, but I'd seen enough weird things in Eerie, Indiana, to know when I was right in the middle of yet another mystery. It was just a matter of time before things started to get *really* strange.

"Let's get out there," said Simon, pulling on his clothes. "I want to try building a snow fort."

I got dressed, too, and both of us went downstairs. My sister and parents were in the kitchen when we got there. My mother was trying to scramble eggs, and they were sticking to the pan.

"Good morning," she said cheerfully. "Would you boys like some eggs?"

I looked at the gloppy mess in the pan and shook my head. "No, thanks," I said. "I'll just have some cereal and toast."

"I'll have eggs, Mrs. Teller," said Simon, sitting down.

My mother smiled. "Well, at least someone around here appreciates a home-cooked breakfast," she said, scraping a pile of eggs onto Simon's plate.

Simon picked up a fork and dug into the eggs. I tried not to watch, but Simon seemed to think my mom's cooking was just great.

"Some storm we got, isn't it?" my father said. "This will probably close the whole town down."

"Yeah," I said. "It's pretty weird. I can't believe how hard it's snowing."

"My guess is a cold front came down from Canada," my dad said. "When it hit the air over Lake Eerie it caused a storm. Nothing so weird about that. It's just nature."

Simon gave me a look over his eggs that said, "See, I told you there was a perfectly normal explanation." I took a bite of toast and ignored him. Maybe my dad was right. But maybe he wasn't.

"I don't know why you're acting so surprised," added my mother. "It's been snowing like this for so long now. Why, I can't even remember when it started."

"Sure," Syndi said. "This storm is a little harder than usual, but I don't see what the big deal is, Mars. You're acting like you've never seen snow before."

"But this is the first snowstorm we've had since we moved to Eerie," I said, looking at them.

My mother laughed. "You're such a kidder," she said. "The first snowstorm. That's a good one."

My father and Syndi started laughing with her, like I'd just made the biggest joke in the world. I looked over at Simon. Suddenly, he didn't seem to be enjoying his eggs so much.

"How long has it been snowing?" I asked.

"Gosh," my father said, putting his paper down. "I don't really remember. Seems like it's always been snowing."

That was when I looked down and noticed his newspaper. It was the *Eerie Examiner,* all right, but the date on the top said DECEMBER 24, 1917.

"Where'd you get that paper?" I asked my father, picking it up and staring at the date.

"Same place I always do," he said. "From the pile in the garage. You know, the ones you use on your paper route. Are you feeling okay, Marshall? You look a little pale."

I wasn't feeling at all right.

"I'm fine," I said. I tucked the paper under my arm and Dad didn't even notice. "I guess I'm just a little bit excited about Christmas. I forgot all about my paper route.''

''You'll have a tough time delivering today,'' my father said. ''Maybe you should try using a sled instead of your bike.''

''Good idea,'' I said. ''In fact, I guess I should get going. You coming, Simon?''

Simon took the hint. ''Sure,'' he said. ''I'll help you pull the . . . um . . . sled.''

We left the kitchen and went back to the Secret Spot. I shut the door and sat down.

''What's going on here?'' asked Simon. ''Why did your parents say it had been snowing forever?''

''I don't know,'' I said. ''But that's not the weirdest thing. Look.''

I showed him the newspaper, which I'd been careful to bring with me.

''Nineteen seventeen!'' Simon said when he saw the date. ''But that's impossible.''

''You're telling me?'' I said. ''The date says it's nineteen seventeen, but the articles and ads are all from today. Something is definitely not right here.''

''How are we going to figure out what it is?'' said Simon.

I thought for a minute. ''First we're going to go on my paper route,'' I said. ''Maybe we'll be able to see exactly what's happened in the rest of Eerie.''

''It's worth a shot,'' said Simon.

We got dressed to go outside, then went into my garage. Sitting on the floor, all wrapped up with rubber bands, were the newspapers for my route. My father was right—there was no way I was going to be able to use my bike. Instead, I took the sled I'd had since I was a little kid down from the wall. It looked a little rusty, but the runners were still sharp, and I figured it would do the job. I put a big cardboard box on the back and filled the box with the papers. Then Simon and I pulled it outside and into the snow.

The blizzard had dumped at least two feet of snow on the streets. Luckily, it was light and fluffy, and while pulling the sled through it was difficult, it wasn't impossible. With Simon's help, I was able to get down the street. At each house, we tossed a paper onto the steps. They sunk right into the snow, so I didn't know how anyone would find them, but at least I was getting the job done.

"Everything looks perfectly normal," said Simon as we made our way down the street and turned the corner. "I mean, all the houses look just the same as they did yesterday. Except for the snow."

"But it's not the same," I said. "Something has to be different."

A minute later, as we turned another corner off Mulder Street and onto Scully Avenue, I found out what was different. At least the first thing. Normally on that corner there's an empty lot. Actually, it's a community garden, a big space filled with plots of vegetables and flowers. In the summer, my mother grows sunflowers there.

But when we turned the corner, there was no garden. Not even an empty lot. Sitting right where the snow-covered remains of Mrs. Pesto's tomato plants should have been was a house. And not just any house. It was the house from the snow globe, the one with the big windows and the young woman inside it.

"Holy crow," said Simon when he looked up and saw the house. "Where did this come from?"

In real life, the house was even more imposing than it was inside the globe. It was three stories tall, with gabled windows and even a sort of rounded tower on one side. It was just sitting there on the lot as though it had been there forever. Even the tree by the front steps looked like it had set down roots and grown there for years and years.

"I knew the globe had something to do with this," I said to Simon.

"What do you mean?"

"This is the house that's inside the snow globe," I said. "At least, it's one of the houses from that town."

"But how did it get *here*?" said Simon. "Houses don't just fall out of the sky."

"Not unless we're in Oz," I said, only half joking. I really did feel as though I'd gone to sleep in one place and woken up in another, just like Dorothy and Toto.

The windows of the house were all shut tight, and curtains were drawn against them so that we couldn't see inside. There was nothing to indicate who lived in the house or whether or not they were still in there.

"In the snow globe this house belongs to a young woman," I said. "She was standing inside looking out. She looked unhappy."

"I wonder if she's in there now," said Simon. "If she is, I'd like to ask her a question or two."

"There's only one way to find out," I said.

Taking a paper out of the box, I trudged through the snow up to the front door. There was no buzzer, but there was a sort of cord hanging down on one side. I took hold of it and tugged. From inside the house, I heard a faint tinkling sound, like the ringing of a bell.

After a minute I heard the sound of feet as someone walked toward the door. There was a series of clicking sounds, like someone unlocking a lot of locks, and then the door opened a crack. A girl's face looked out, but it wasn't the woman from the snow globe. The girl looked just a little older than me.

"What is it?" she said.

"I brought the morning paper," I said, waving the *Examiner* at her. "I didn't want to just leave it in the snow."

The girl opened the door wider, and I saw that she was wearing a white apron over a plain blue dress.

There was a small hat on her head, and she was carrying a feather duster. She looked like a maid.

"Thank you very much," she said, taking the paper from me. "I'm sure that Miss will be very grateful for having a dry paper this morning."

I looked past the girl and into the hall. The house was beautiful, but it seemed very much out of date. The wooden floors were covered in thick rugs, and the furniture looked as if it belonged in an antique shop, only it sparkled as though it were almost new. The wood shone darkly, and the wallpaper was covered in intricate designs. A huge grandfather clock stood at the foot of the stairs.

My eyes traveled up the stairway to the landing. There on the wall was an oil painting of a young man. He was very handsome, and he was wearing what looked like a soldier's uniform. As I was staring at it, I saw someone start to come down the stairs from the second floor. I saw a pair of feet on the stairs, and above them the edge of a dress.

"Lucy, who is it?" said a quiet voice. "Has the mail arrived yet?"

The maid turned around. "It's just the paper boy," she said. "No one important."

She turned back to me. "You must go now," she said. "It won't do to have Miss disturbed. There's so much to do."

Lucy reached into her pocket and pulled something

out. She held it out to me, and I took it. Then she turned away and shut the door before I could get a glimpse of the face of the person coming down the stairs. I heard the locks clicking shut again, and then the sound of Lucy's feet rushing off into the house.

I stared at the door for another minute. I was tempted to ring the bell again and see if I could get into the house, but I decided to wait. Instead I went back down the steps to where Simon stood waiting.

"What did you see?" he asked.

"Not much," I told him. "Mainly a painting of some guy and then someone's feet coming down the stairs. I still don't know whose house it is."

"I saw that girl hand you something," said Simon. "What was it?"

I'd been so intent on seeing inside the house that I hadn't even looked at what Lucy had given me. Now I opened my hand and looked. Laying on my palm was a coin.

"She tipped me," I said.

I looked at the coin. At first I thought it was just a regular dime. But when I looked more closely, I saw that it wasn't. I held it up. On one side there was a picture of a woman holding what looked like a bundle of leaves. On the other side was a picture of an eagle.

"Wow!" said Simon, taking it from me. "Do you know what this is?"

"A dime?" I said.

"No. This is a penny. But not just any penny. This is a nineteen seventeen Victory penny. They only made them during World War I. They were made out of tin because metal was needed for the war. After the war, they melted them all down again and turned them into cans for vegetables. You almost never see them. But this one looks brand-new."

I looked back at the house. I wondered what secrets were hiding inside its walls. Whoever was in there, I knew she was somehow responsible for the blizzard, and for whatever else was going on.

As I was turning to go, I noticed something move in one of the third-floor windows. Someone was watching us from up there. I covered my eyes with my hand and tried to see through the snow. But whoever it was must have seen me, because all I caught was a flash of curtain closing and then the window was empty again.

3

"She was looking at us," I said, pointing to the window.

"Who was?" said Simon, still looking at the Victory penny.

"The woman from inside the house," I said. "I didn't see her face, but I know it's the same woman from the house in the snow globe. It has to be."

"But why would her house just suddenly appear here?" asked Simon. "None of the other houses from the snow globe village did."

"Not that we know of," I said. "I think we should take a look around town and see if anything else weird has turned up during the blizzard."

Leaving the sled behind, we plodded through the snow and made our way into the center of town. All over Eerie, people were outside in the snow. Some of them had attempted to shovel out their driveways or their sidewalks, but the snow was falling so heavily that as soon as they tossed a shovelful of it away, the empty space left behind was filling up again. Most people had simply given up and gone inside, or else were busy building snowmen and making snow angels.

A couple of people were having a snowball fight, flinging snowballs across the street at one another. One hit me on the side of the head, filling my ear with cold snow.

"Hey!" I shouted. "Who did that?"

A head popped up from behind a snow-covered bush. "Sorry about that, little paper boy," said the King.

I scooped up a handful of snow and packed it into a loose ball. Before the King could duck, I sent it sailing at him. It hit him right in the middle of his forehead, where his black hair dipped down in a curl.

"Bull's-eye!" crowed Simon, and we both cracked up laughing.

That started another round in the snowball battle, and soon the air was filled with flying missiles. Ducking under the barrage of snowballs being fired back and forth across the street, Simon and I walked the rest of the way into town. Even though the streets were packed with snow, people were still going about their Christmas Eve activities. It was as if no one thought the sudden blizzard was odd at all—like this sort of thing happened every day in Eerie.

We made it to World of Stuff and went inside. Mr. Radford was handing out hot chocolate and doughnuts.

"Well, well, well," he said when he saw us. "If it

isn't my two best customers. Merry day before Christmas." Then he leaned down and whispered to us, "Thanks for letting me in on this Christmas thing, boys. People really seem to be going for it. I should do it more often."

"No problem," I said, taking a cup of cocoa. "Say, Mr. Radford, how long has it been snowing now?"

"Snowing?" said Mr. Radford. "Is it snowing?" He ran to the front door and looked outside. "Good heavens," he said. "I guess it is. I hadn't noticed."

"So you don't know when it started?" asked Simon as he munched on a jelly doughnut.

Mr. Radford rubbed his head thoughtfully. "Can't say as I recall," he said. "Then again, I don't remember a time when it *wasn't* snowing."

Chief Hoffa, the head of the Eerie Police, was sitting at the counter eating doughnuts and drinking cocoa. He'd heard our conversation, and he joined in.

"What a question," he said. "When did it start snowing? Why, it's *always* been snowing, at least as long as I can remember."

Simon and I exchanged glances. Something was definitely not right.

"So this blizzard didn't just suddenly happen?" I asked Chief Hoffa.

"Don't be ridiculous," he said, snorting. "Next thing, you'll be telling me Eerie is populated with aliens or something."

"Well, actually . . . " Simon began to say, but I stepped on his foot to make him shut up.

I decided to ask another question. "Do you happen to know who lives in that house on the corner of Mulder and Scully? The one with the big windows."

Chief Hoffa scrunched up his forehead. "Let me see," he said, thinking. "I know just about everyone in Eerie. I'm sure I know who lives there."

Simon and I watched his face as he thought. Several times he looked like he was about to say something, but each time he opened his mouth and then stopped, as though he'd forgotten what it was he was going to say. Finally he shook his head. "You know, I can't say I recall who does live there," he said. "But I know that house has been there forever. I'm sure it will come to me later. Maybe if I have another doughnut."

He helped himself to another doughnut and began to munch happily. He didn't seem the slightest bit interested in the strange house or anything else. He just opened up the newspaper in front of him and started reading.

A minute later, the door opened and in ran Mrs. Marlowe, the B. F. Skinner Junior High drama teacher. As usual, she seemed to be in a panic about something. Her curly red hair was bundled up in a scarf, and her glasses were all fogged up from the cold. She was trying to look over them, but she still kept bumping into things.

"Oh, my," she said as she collided with a display of

Eerie postcards. "I have so much to do, and so little time. Here it is Christmas Eve, and I'm just not ready."

"Hi, Mrs. Marlowe," said Simon.

Mrs. Marlowe stared at us through her fogged-up glasses. When she couldn't figure out who we were, she took them off, rubbed them with her scarf, and put them back on.

"Ah," she said. "Simon and Marshall. Just the boys I was looking for."

"You were?" I said. "For us?"

"Yes," she said, taking each of us by a hand. "I need some help putting together the pageant."

"Pageant?" said Simon.

She sighed. "The Christmas pageant," she said. "The one we're putting on this afternoon at the town hall. I need you boys to help me sct up and keep the little ones organized."

I hadn't heard anything about a pageant. I started to protest, but before I knew it, Mrs. Marlowe had somehow gotten us out the door and onto the street. Simon was still holding a half-eaten doughnut in his hand.

"There's so much to do," Mrs. Marlowe said as she shepherded us toward the town hall. "We need to finish painting the sets and getting the costumes together. Do either of you know how to play the piano?"

"No," I said.

"Darn," said Mrs. Marlowe. "I need someone to

play 'We Three Kings' as the wise men walk down the aisle. Oh, well, we'll think of something.''

When we reached the auditorium of the town hall, I saw that it was filled with kids. They were running around and screaming, chasing each other through the rows of seats. Some of them were dressed in what looked like their fathers' old bathrobes. A few had on paper angel wings that flapped and bobbled behind them as they ran.

Mrs. Marlowe climbed onto the auditorium stage. She put her fingers in her mouth and gave a piercing whistle. Almost immediately, the kids stopped running around and just stood in place, staring at her.

"All right, now," she said. "Listen up. We have a lot to do before five o'clock.''

She pointed at Simon. "You. Take these children over there and make sure they have their costumes on properly. I don't want to see any shepherds with angel wings or sheep wearing crowns—is that clear?''

All the kids nodded.

"Good. Now, you.'' She pointed at me. "I need you to help finish painting the stable set.''

Simon went over to where the children were milling around. I followed Mrs. Marlowe. She took me behind the stage and handed me a paintbrush and some cans of paint. She pointed to a half-finished backdrop that looked like the inside of a stable.

"There you go," she said. "Make it look good. I'll be back to check on you.''

She disappeared through the curtains, and I was left staring at the set. I looked at the paintbrush in my hand. I'd never painted anything in my life. Still, there was no one else to do it, so I got to work. Much to my surprise, once I got started, I was kind of into it. It was fun.

I was just finishing up the last details on a pile of hay in the manger when Mrs. Marlowe came back.

"Marshall, that's just perfect," she said. "I had no idea you were such an artist."

"Well," I said. "I didn't know, either."

Mrs. Marlowe beamed. "Now go out and help Simon," she said. "He's not having such an easy time of it."

I went back to the auditorium and saw that things were totally out of control. The kids were tearing around again, and Simon was frantically waving his arms and calling for them to stop. When he saw me, he ran over.

"Mars, you've got to help," he said. "The angels are going insane, and Mary and Joseph are missing."

"Relax," I said. "We can do this."

I stopped a herd of angels that were running by me and told them to sit down. Then I had all the kids dressed as sheep move to one part of the auditorium. Before long, everyone was in order, and we got started with the rehearsal.

Things went really smoothly. Mrs. Marlowe had found a girl who could sort of play the piano, and she banged out the familiar songs as the kids acted out the pageant. The whole thing only took about half an hour.

"I can't thank you enough," said Mrs. Marlowe as the kids filed back into the dressing room area.

"Anytime," I said.

Mrs. Marlowe went to check on the kids, and Simon and I were alone.

"How'd we get into this, anyway?" asked Simon.

"I'm not sure," I said. "It probably has something to do with the snow globe, but I have no idea how they're connected. All we can do is wait and see."

For the next two hours, we were busy helping Mrs. Marlowe get all the last details of the pageant in order. A little before five, people started arriving for the pageant, and pretty soon the whole auditorium was filled with people from Eerie.

"This is so strange," said Simon, peeking out from behind the stage curtains. "They're all sitting there like this is all supposed to be happening."

"They probably think it is," I said.

Just then, Mrs. Marlowe ran up to us. "Boys," she said. "Two of the shepherds just threw up and can't go on. They ate too many cookies. You'll have to take their places."

She thrust two bathrobes into our hands and handed us some long wooden sticks. "Don't forget your crooks," she said, and disappeared again.

Before we could say anything, the lights dimmed and the wavering sounds of the piano filled the room. The curtain started to go up, and we had to hurry and pull the bathrobes on before everyone saw us. When the curtain finally rose, we were standing in the middle of the stage, surrounded by six little kids dressed as sheep.

"B—a—a—a," said the little kids in chorus, and waggled their ears.

I looked out at the audience. I had no idea what to do, so I poked one of the sheep with my staff, the way I thought a real shepherd would.

"Hey," whispered the little kid. "Cut it out."

I was saved by the appearance of the angels being pushed onstage by Mrs. Marlowe. They shuffled out to the applause of the audience, and the piano player began playing "Hark, the Herald Angels Sing."

I looked out at the audience again, and this time I gasped. Sitting a few rows from the front was the lady from the snow globe. She was all wrapped up in a black coat trimmed with fur, and she wore a black hat with a long feather in it. The feather was tickling the face of the man behind her, and he kept trying to brush it away from his nose.

I had to get Simon's attention, but he wasn't looking at me, and there were two sheep between us.

"Simon," I hissed, but he didn't hear me because the piano was too loud.

I moved a little bit closer to him, edging around one of the sheep.

"Hey, you're blocking me," said the sheep. "My mom can't see me."

33

I ignored her and moved behind the second sheep until I was right near Simon.

"Simon," I whispered again.

This time he heard me, and turned around.

"What?" he hissed back.

"The woman in the third row," I said as quietly as I could. "In the black coat. That's the woman from the house. We have to try and talk to her."

"We can't just leave," said Simon. "We'll have to wait until the pageant is over. Watch out. Here come the wise men."

For the next twenty minutes I tried to sneak glances at the woman in black whenever I could. Once I almost tripped a wise man as he went up to see the baby Jesus.

"Watch it, dummy," he said as he righted his crown.

Finally it was over. The piano player launched into "Silent Night," and the audience began to applaud wildly. As soon as the curtain went down, I grabbed Simon and we rushed off the stage and out into the hallway.

When we got into the auditorium, the place was swarming with parents putting on their coats and looking for their kids. I tried to find the woman in black, but she was gone.

Then I saw the feather from her hat. It was bobbing along above the crowd as she moved toward the back doors. I started pushing through the sea of parents, trying to follow her. I was getting closer to her when someone stepped in front of me. It was Chief Hoffa.

"Good work, boys," he said. "Best darn shepherds I've ever seen. Almost made me cry."

"Thanks," I said, craning my head around to find the woman in black. But she was nowhere to be seen. I'd lost her.

"It's no use," I said to Simon. "She's gone."

"Why was she even here?" he said. "What does she have to do with a Christmas pageant?"

"It looks like we won't find out," I said.

Just then, Mrs. Marlowe came up to us. "Some of us are going to go out caroling tonight, boys," she said. "How would you like to come along?"

I started to say no, but then I remembered something. "We'd love to," I said. "What time?"

"About seven," said Mrs. Marlowe. "We're leaving from World of Stuff."

"We'll be there," I said, and she left to go talk to some other people.

"Why'd you tell her we'd go?" Simon complained. "You know I can't sing."

"Carolers," I said. "In the snow globe, there are carolers outside the woman's house. If we go with them, maybe we can get inside."

Simon groaned. "Okay," he said. "But I am *not* singing."

4

As it turned out, Simon *did* sing. So did I. We really didn't have a choice.

We met Mrs. Marlowe and the other carolers at World of Stuff, just as she told us to. About an hour before, it had started to snow even harder, and the wind was blowing the snow all around in great sweeping swirls that looked like dancing ghosts. We'd put on extra clothes and had thick scarves wrapped around our necks to keep out the cold. Even so, it was freezing.

"I can't believe we're going to walk around in this," said Simon as we stamped our feet to keep warm. "This is crazy."

"I'm telling you, I think this is important," I said. "These carolers have something to do with the woman in black."

"Well, I told my mom that I'd be back by nine," said Simon. "We always open one present before Christmas morning."

"Don't worry," I said. "I have to be home, too. We

36

always decorate the tree on Christmas Eve, and when I left, my dad was setting it up in the living room. By the time I get back, he should have tripped over the lights about six times."

"This is the weirdest Christmas ever," said Simon. Little did he know, the weirdness was just beginning.

As soon as everyone arrived, Mrs. Marlowe had us stand in one group and practice before we went out to entertain the town. I ended up standing between Simon and the King, who was warming up by shaking his hips and saying "Thank you very much" about once every ten seconds.

"I love carols, don't you, little paper boy?" he said.

"Sure," I said weakly. Singing has never been one of my strong points, and I really didn't want to sing in front of other people.

Mrs. Marlowe started out by having us sing "Oh, Christmas Tree." I tried to sing softly so that no one would hear me. Luckily, Chief Hoffa sang loudly enough to drown out almost everyone around him.

We practiced maybe four or five carols before Mrs. Marlowe decided we were ready to take our show on the road. Then we all marched out into the blizzard and started making our way through the streets of Eerie, singing our hearts out.

Wherever we went, the wind blew against us, even when we turned corners and it should have been blowing the other direction. It was as if all of Eerie were surrounded by a circling storm that was trying to keep us from celebrating Christmas Eve. Snowflakes just kept tumbling out of the sky, quickly covering my coat in a skin of snow. If I hadn't kept wiping myself off, I would have looked like a walking, singing snowman.

But nobody seemed to mind the cold or the snow. They were all singing like crazy, their voices filling the night sky with the jolly sounds of Christmas. Before long even I was singing a little bit louder, caught up in the excitement.

At each house we went to, the people inside opened their doors and came out onto their steps or their front porches to listen to us sing. A couple even decided to join us, and by the time we'd gone down Main Street, there was quite a big group of carolers.

When we reached the end of Mulder Street, we were just finishing up the last chorus of "It Came Upon a Midnight Clear." When the last note died away, Mrs. Marlowe cleared her throat.

"Okay," she said. "Let's make this next song a really good one."

"How about 'All I Want for Christmas is My Two Front Teeth?' " suggested Chief Hoffa.

"Thank you for the suggestion, Jimmy," said Mrs. Marlowe. "But I was thinking of something slightly more traditional."

She hummed a note for us and then launched into "O, Holy Night," her high voice soaring above our heads. We all joined in, and we walked to the front of the strange house on Scully Avenue and waited for the door to open.

At all the other houses the doors had opened very quickly, as soon as the people inside heard us singing. But the door to the house on Scully Avenue stayed firmly shut. Not only that, but all of the windows were dark. No candles burned inside. No cheerful wreaths hung on the windows. No heartwarming Christmas scenes were visible through the big panes of glass.

"Do you think she's gone?" Simon asked me.

"No," I said. "I think she's hiding inside. For some reason she doesn't want to come out."

I scanned the windows of the house, looking for any sign of the woman in black. I was hoping that I could catch a glimpse of her peering out at us, as I had the first time we'd been there. But the windows remained empty, like blind eyes staring back at me.

"Well," said Mrs. Marlowe when the song ended and there was still no sign of the woman in black. "It seems that *someone* isn't in the Christmas mood tonight."

"Maybe we should just go," suggested Mr. Radford.

"Or maybe we should try harder," said Mrs. Marlowe. "I will not go home until every last person in Eerie has received a taste of holiday joy. After all, this is Christmas!"

She began to sing an enthusiastic rendition of "We

Wish You a Merry Christmas." She was waving her hands in the air, trying to get us to sing more loudly. Pretty soon I felt as though I was shouting the words instead of singing them.

"Bring us some figgy pudding!" we warbled, our breath making clouds in the cold air. "We won't go until we get some!"

Suddenly, the front door opened and Lucy appeared in the doorway. She looked very distraught. Her hair was flying loose from her cap, and she was wringing her hands as she motioned for us to be quiet.

"Please," she said plaintively. "Please go away."

Mrs. Marlowe stopped singing immediately and stared openmouthed at Lucy. "Go away?" she said. "You mean just like that?"

Lucy nodded. "Please," she said. "Don't make it any worse for her."

Mrs. Marlowe snorted. "Well, I can see when we're not wanted," she said. "We're sorry to have bothered you."

With that, she started to walk away down the street to the next house. The rest of the carolers followed her, but I held on to Simon's elbow and motioned for him to stay behind.

"Wait a minute," I said. "This is our chance to find out what's going on."

Lucy was just closing the big front door as we ran up the steps.

"Wait!" I called out. "Just a minute."

She looked at us. If she remembered us from earlier in the morning, she didn't let on.

"What do you want?" she said angrily. "I haven't any figgy pudding for you."

"No, no," I said. "We don't want any figgy pudding—whatever that is. We just want to talk to you. We want to know what's happened here."

"That is none of your concern," she said, and started to shut the door.

"But the lady," I said. "Who is she? And why won't she come out?"

"As I said before," said Lucy firmly, "that is none of your concern. Now please leave us alone. A great tragedy has taken place, and we must be alone. Now, good night."

She pushed the door closed and I heard her lock it up tightly.

"Merry Christmas to you, too," I said to the closed door.

"Now what?" said Simon.

"There's not much we can do," I said. "We're not getting into that house, that's for sure. She's got it locked up tight. All we can do is go home. We'll have to see what happens next."

"Well, tomorrow is Christmas, anyway," said Simon. "At least that will be fun. I'm sure this mystery can wait one day."

I smiled. "You're probably right," I said.

Mrs. Marlowe and the other carolers had made their way down the block and were already at the next corner. I could barely see them through the blinding snow, but Chief Hoffa was carrying a flashlight, and its thin yellow light played over the ground. I almost considered catching up with them, but then I saw that I only had a few minutes to get home for the family Christmas Eve activities. So Simon and I took a shortcut down Jackson Street until we came to our own street. In each house we passed, there were families trimming trees, opening gifts, and watching Christmas specials on television.

"Well," I said when we reached our houses. "I guess that's it for tonight. I'll see you tomorrow and we can compare notes about the presents we got."

"Great," said Simon. "Maybe I'll get that new telescope and we can finally see what those lights are over the cemetery."

"Right," I said. "And maybe I'll get the video camera and we can finally catch Bigfoot on tape."

"Or maybe we'll both get clothes," said Simon.

"Don't say that," I said. "The last thing I need is another turtleneck sweater."

"Good luck," said Simon. "Merry Christmas."

"You too," I answered. "Merry Christmas."

I was inside my house before I remembered that I'd forgotten to give Simon his Christmas present. "Oh well," I thought. "I can always give it to him tomorrow."

As I'd suspected, my father was in the living room, attempting to put the lights on the Christmas tree. He'd somehow managed to wrap most of the string around his legs, and he was trying to get untangled when I walked in.

"Hey, Mars," he said. "You're just in time to help with the tree."

"I don't know, Dad," I joked. "It looks like you have everything under control here."

I helped get him free from the lights, and together we put them all around the tree, just as we did every year. Within fifteen minutes, the tree sparkled with red, blue, and green lights.

"Perfect," said my mother, coming in with boxes of ornaments. Syndi was right behind her, carrying even more boxes. They put them on the coffee table.

"How was caroling?" my mother asked me.

"Okay," I said. "A little cold. It's really blowing around out there."

"It's been picking up all night," my father said. "That wind must really be blowing hard from Canada."

"Well, we're all inside now," said my mother. "It's Christmas Eve, and we have a tree to decorate. Let's get to it."

For the next hour we hung ornament after ornament on the tree. It seemed like each one had its own story about how it had been made or where my mother had bought it, and she insisted on telling each story again, even though we'd heard them a dozen times before. Finally, the tree was done and we all sat down to look at it.

"It's the prettiest tree ever," said Syndi.

"You say that every year," I said, teasing her.

"And every year I'm right," she said.

The clock over the fireplace chimed eleven.

"Wow, it's late," my father said. "You two had better get to bed, or Santa won't be able to bring any presents."

"Oh, Dad," said Syndi and I together. We're both way too old to believe in Santa Claus, but still my dad says this every year.

"Now off to bed with you two," my mother said. "Tomorrow is a busy day."

Syndi and I went upstairs to our rooms. Every year it was the same thing—my parents waited until we were asleep before they put out our gifts. Then, on Christmas morning, we'd run downstairs and pretend to be surprised. It was silly, but I had to admit that it was kind of fun.

In my room, I put on my pajamas and got into bed. As I was turning out the light, I remembered that I'd forgotten to wrap my mother's gift. I looked at it sitting on my desk. Inside the globe the snowstorm was blowing so hard that I couldn't even see the miniature village. I looked outside my window and saw that it was blowing just as hard around my house. For a brief moment I thought about picking up the globe and smashing it to the floor to see what would happen. But I knew I wouldn't do it. I wanted too much to know what was going on in Eerie, and I knew the snow globe was the key.

Instead, I pulled the covers up tight. I listened to the wind howling around my house, its low voice singing a sad, cold song about winter. The song filled my head, and before long I fell asleep.

When I woke up, it was morning. A thin, gray light was shining in my window. Outside, the storm had let up. The snow was still falling, but not as hard or as angrily. It seemed almost normal.

Remembering that it was Christmas morning, I jumped out of bed and ran downstairs. I always like to be the first one up on Christmas morning. I tore down the stairs and ran into the living room. It was empty. There was no tree. No presents. Nothing.

I ran into the kitchen, sure that someone was playing a joke on me. My father was sitting at the table, reading the paper. My mother was looking in the refrigerator.

"What's going on?" I demanded to know.

My father put down his paper. "What do you mean, Marshall?"

"I mean where's the tree? Where are the presents?"

My parents looked at me strangely, as though I'd said something totally crazy.

"It's Christmas!" I said. "You know—the day we open all those presents. Am I missing something?"

My father started to laugh. "I'm afraid you're a little bit ahead of yourself, son," he said.

Now it was my turn to look at him like he was the crazy one. "What are you talking about?"

"You're a day early," my mother said, pouring some milk into a glass.

"Huh?"

"Christmas is tomorrow," my father said. "Not today."

I couldn't believe what I was hearing. I *knew* that it was Christmas morning. There was no way it couldn't be. We'd decorated the tree. I'd gone caroling. Now I was supposed to be opening boxes and throwing away the paper and bows.

Something was very wrong. I picked up the paper my father had put on the table and looked at the front page. There, across the top, was the date in black and white: DECEMBER 24, 1917.

I was living the same day over again.

5

I just stood there for a minute, staring at the date on the paper. I even closed my eyes and opened them again, thinking that maybe the date would have changed in the few seconds that I wasn't looking at it.

"Are you sure this is today's paper?" I asked my father. "It isn't yesterday's?"

"Of course it's today's," he said. "I think I know what day it is. Besides, I just took it from the pile in the garage. Which reminds me, you'd better get busy on your paper route. There's a lot of snow out there. If you don't get going, it *will* be Christmas before you're finished."

I sank into one of the kitchen chairs, the paper still in my hand. I looked down at the date on my watch and saw the tiny numbers: 24.

"Are you okay, Marshall?" asked my mother. She came over and put her hand on my forehead. "You're not coming down with something, are you? I'd hate for you to be sick on Christmas."

"Oh, uh, I'm fine," I said. "I must have just dreamed that it was Christmas or something. I guess I'm a little excited, is all."

"I would be, too, if I were you," said my dad. "Especially since I know what you're getting."

"Now, Edgar, you keep quiet," my mother said, swatting him with a dish towel. "And you, get going on your route," she said to me. "That snow is falling hard out there."

I nodded, left the kitchen, and went back up to my room. I was still sort of in shock over what was going on. Somehow, I'd lived through an entire day, only to wake up and find that none of it had happened. Or at least that no one else remembered that it had happened.

That's when I thought of Simon. I had to talk to him. If he remembered everything that had happened the day before, then it couldn't have been a dream. But if he didn't remember it, then maybe it meant that I was making all of it—the caroling, the house, the pageant, the woman in black, all of it—up. Even worse, maybe it meant that I was going crazy. I had to find out.

I pulled on some clothes as quickly as I could. As I tied my shoes, I noticed the globe on my desk. The snowstorm had settled down. Now only a few bits of the fake snow were moving around in the water. I went over and picked the globe up. Inside, the village looked calm and peaceful. In the woman's house, no one was looking out the windows.

"I'm going to find out who you are," I said to her through the glass, wondering if she could hear me through the water. I wasn't sure, but I thought that maybe, just for a split second, I saw a shadow move behind one of the third-floor windows.

Putting the globe down, I went downstairs and out the back door, pulling on my coat, gloves, hat, and scarf as I went. I needed to do my paper route, but I had to speak to Simon first. I waded next door and knocked on his door. He opened it almost immediately.

"Hi," I said. I wasn't sure what to say next. If Simon didn't remember the day before, I didn't want him to think I was hallucinating or something.

"Hi," he said. He seemed to be looking at me kind of oddly.

"Did you have a good night last night?" I said, hoping he would say something that would let me know where he thought he'd been.

"Yeah," he said. "It was a lot of fun. How about you?"

"It was okay," I said. I decided to take a risk. "Some of the songs were hard to sing."

Simon let out a big sigh. "Man, am I glad you said that. So we *were* out caroling last night, right? I didn't make it all up?"

"It was real, all right," I said. "I was afraid you wouldn't remember."

"You should have seen the look on my mother's face

when I gave her a present this morning," Simon said. "Once I figured out what was going on, I had to pretend I'd gotten her two gifts, one for today and one for tomorrow. Now I have to find her something else for Christmas."

"If it ever comes," I said. "From the look of things, we're stuck in December twenty-fourth."

"Do you have any idea why?" asked Simon.

"Not yet," I said. "But I have a pretty good idea who's behind it. I think it's time we found out more about that lady in black."

"But we can't get into the house," Simon said. "And Lucy won't talk to us. Where else can we go?"

"Back to where this all started," I said. "World of Stuff."

I went inside and waited while Simon got dressed.

"Did you do the whole tree-trimming thing last night, too?" I asked.

"Yeah," said Simon. "I almost freaked when I came downstairs this morning and it was all gone. I felt like little Cindy Lou Hoo in *How the Grinch Stole Christmas*. I was sure someone had come in the middle of the night and taken it all away."

I laughed. "I know how you felt," I said.

Simon grabbed his coat, and we went back outside.

"Aren't you going to do your paper route?" Simon asked.

I shook my head. "There's no time," I said. "Besides, they read it all yesterday."

Just like the day before, the streets were filled with people playing in the snow. Only this time I wasn't having much fun watching them. It was like seeing a really cool movie for the second time, only you don't jump at the scary parts or laugh at the funny parts because you've already seen them before. And this was worse, because it was real. I felt like I knew everything that was going to happen, so that when we walked by the King's house, for example, I ducked, even though he wasn't there to throw a snowball at me.

"This is too strange," I said to Simon. "I keep expecting the same things to happen that happened yesterday, only they don't."

"I know," he said. "It's like this is the same day, but the same things aren't happening."

"I don't know what would be worse," I said, "living the same exact events over and over again or always having it be the day before Christmas without ever actually having Christmas."

"Let's hope we don't have to find out," Simon said.

When we got to World of Stuff, Mr. Radford was once again serving doughnuts and hot chocolate. And once again, Chief Hoffa was sitting at the counter. But different people were shopping, and this time the doughnuts were cinnamon instead of jelly filled.

"Well, well, well, if it isn't my two best customers,"

Mr. Radford said, just as he had the day before. "What can I do for you boys today?"

"We were just wondering," I said. "Do you happen to remember where you got that snow globe that I bought here the other day?"

"Snow globe?" Mr. Radford said. "I'm not sure I remember a snow globe."

"I found it in a box back there," I said, pointing to the rear of the store. "The box was mainly filled with old Christmas ornaments."

Mr. Radford thought for a minute. "Ornaments?" he said. "Box? Oh, you mean that big cardboard box."

"That's the one!" Simon said.

Mr. Radford smiled. "Isn't that a beauty?" he said. "Don't make boxes like that anymore. I knew right when I saw it that I wanted it. Real craftsmanship."

"We're not really interested in the box," I said. "I mean, it is a great box and all. But we're really more interested in what's inside it."

"Oh," said Mr. Radford. "Well, I can't say as I ever really looked inside it. Is there good stuff in there?"

I nodded. "We like it. Do you remember where you got it?"

"Let me see," he said. "Where did I get that box?" He scratched his head for a minute. Then he held his hand up, one finger pointing toward the ceiling. "I've got it! I remember now. I got that box at an estate auction over in Shady Corners. Paid a good price for it, too. Had to outbid some fella from the big city for it. Some hotshot antique dealer. Bet he already has a lot of great boxes.''

"Great," I said. "Whose estate was it?"

"Estate?" said Mr. Radford. "Oh, I don't know. There was a lot of stuff from all over. Could be anybody's."

"Great," I said again, although this time I was being sarcastic. "Now we'll never figure out who it belongs to."

"Belongs to?" said Mr. Radford. "Why? Is someone asking for it back? I paid good money for that box, I tell you. Good money. I'm not giving it—"

"No," I said. "No one wants it back. We're just curious to know who the snow globe belonged to."

"Oh, is that all?" Mr. Radford said. "Well, why not just look through the box? Maybe there's something else in there that would give you a clue."

"Good idea," said Simon. "We'll do that. Mr. Radford, you're a genius."

"A genie?" he said as we went to the back of the store. "I don't think I want to be a genie. Those lamps look awfully cramped."

We found the box sitting right where we'd left it. No one else seemed to be interested in it, and it looked as though it hadn't even been opened since we'd been there. We knelt down on the floor and opened the top.

Inside, the old ornaments were all still carefully

wrapped. We took them out one by one and laid them on the floor, out of the way so that nobody would step on them. The box was filled with them, and soon there was a big pile around our feet.

"I don't think there's anything else in here," I said dejectedly as I took out what seemed to be the eightieth glass ball or piece of glass fruit.

Then I picked up another paper-wrapped ball and saw something underneath. It was a bundle of papers, and it was tied together with a lavender silk ribbon.

"What's that?" asked Simon.

I picked up the pile and looked at it. "It looks like a stack of letters," I said.

I pulled gently on the end of the string and the bow holding it opened up. The ribbon slipped away from the letters, and I stuck it into my pocket. I took the first letter and looked at the writing on the envelope. The ink was faded to a light brown, and the handwriting was spidery, but I could make out that it was addressed to Miss Prudence Lively. There was no return address. The postmark was from November, 1917.

I flipped quickly through the stack of letters. They were all addressed to Miss Prudence Lively of Shady Corners, and all of them were addressed in the same spidery handwriting.

"Well, I don't know who wrote these letters," I said. "But whoever it was wrote a lot of them."

I was looking through the envelopes when I found

something else. Tucked in between some of the letters was a handful of pictures. Like the ink on the envelopes, these, too, had faded to a light brown color. They were printed on heavy paper, almost like cardboard.

I put the letters down and showed Simon the photos. The first one was a picture of some people in an old car. They were waving at the camera, but I couldn't make out any of their faces. I turned to the next photo.

"That's her," I exclaimed when I saw it. "That's the woman in black."

The picture we were looking at showed a beautiful young woman standing on the steps of a house—the same house as in the snow globe and in the lot on Scully Avenue. She was wearing a pretty white dress and a big hat covered with flowers. Her hair was tied back with a ribbon, and she was smiling sweetly at the camera.

"She looks so happy," said Simon.

"That must be Prudence Lively," I said. It felt good to have a name to go with the face of the woman in black, as if one small piece of the puzzle had fallen into place.

I turned to the next picture. It showed Prudence sitting on a blanket in the grass. Sitting next to her was a young man. He was wearing a white suit and a straw hat. He was trying to feed Prudence a strawberry, and she was laughing and pushing his hand away.

"Look how much fun they're having," I said.

"But who is he?" said Simon.

I had no idea. I turned the photo over, but there was nothing written on the back to indicate who the man was.

The last picture in the pile showed the same young man. Only this time he was wearing a uniform of some kind. His pants and shirt looked clean and pressed, and he had a small hat on his head. He was standing on what looked like a dock, and Prudence was standing next to him. He had his arm around her, but she didn't look happy. Her eyes were sad, and her mouth seemed to refuse to smile.

"I wonder what's happening," said Simon.

I looked at the letters. "I don't know," I said, wrapping the lavender ribbon around them and slipping them into my pocket along with the photographs, "but I think if we read them we'll find some answers."

6

After putting the packet of letters and photographs into my pocket, I turned and walked out of World of Stuff, waving to Mr. Radford as we passed by.

"Merry Christmas," he said.

"Merry Christmas," Simon and I said at the same time.

As we went out onto the street, I saw Mrs. Marlowe coming up the sidewalk. She was waving at us and saying something I couldn't quite hear.

"Hurry," I said to Simon. "If she catches us, we'll end up in that horrible pageant again. I don't know about you, but the last thing I want to do again is stand there in some old bathrobe while those sheep kids baa around me."

"I'm with you," said Simon.

We headed in the opposite direction from Mrs. Marlowe, jumping over a big snowbank and walking down the street as quickly as possible. For once, I was glad I'd known what was going to happen.

"Do you think Mr. Radford will miss those letters?" Simon asked.

"I doubt it. If he never even opened the box, he probably won't care. Besides, I think what we're doing is more important."

"What exactly *are* we doing?" said Simon.

"I'm hoping there will be some kind of clue in one of the letters," I said. "Something that will tell us what happened to Prudence Lively, and who that man in the photographs is. I've got a feeling he's somehow connected to the snow globe."

"I hope we figure it all out pretty soon," said Simon. "I like Christmas and all, but this is getting ridiculous."

"Look at the bright side," I said. "As long as it's always December twenty-fourth, there won't be any school."

When we got back to my house, we left our snow-covered coats in the kitchen and went up to the Secret Spot. I was glad to get out of the snow and sit somewhere warm and dry.

Taking the letters out of my pocket, I spread them out on my desk. They all looked pretty much the same, each one addressed in the same handwriting and the same colored ink. But by looking at the postmarks, it was easy to arrange them in order by date. Altogether, there were a dozen or so letters. The four pictures I put aside.

I picked up the first envelope. The top had been neatly opened, like whoever read it had used a letter opener, and it was easy to slide out the sheet of paper inside. The paper itself was very thin, and it was covered on one side in the same handwriting that was on the outside. I held it close and read:

September 17, 1917

Dearest Prudence:

    I have been here at camp for only two days, and already I miss your smiling face. I think of you often as I go through my daily routine. The work is hard, but I am sure it will make me a fine soldier. They need as many of us as they can get over there, and I am glad to do my part. My only regret is that it takes me away from you.

    I do not have much time before lights out, so I will say only that I miss you and that I love you. I am counting the days until I can return to you and we can be married. Until then, I carry your picture with me always in my shirt pocket, where it is close to my heart.

Yours always,
Henry

"Well, that explains the picture of the man in the uniform," said Simon when we were finished reading.

"This Henry guy must have been her fiancé, and he joined the army or something."

"Well, in nineteen seventeen, World War One was going on," I said, remembering what I'd learned in Miss Earhart's history class at B. F. Skinner Junior High. "This was written a few months after the United States joined the war. It would make sense if he was in the army then."

"Open the next letter," said Simon.

"I feel weird reading their personal letters," I said. "I don't think Henry would be too thrilled if he knew we were reading his love notes to his girlfriend."

"It's for a good cause," said Simon. "I'm sure he'd understand."

I put the first letter away and opened the next one. It was dated only a few days after the first one, and was filled mainly with boring descriptions of the training that Henry was getting. In it he complained about the awful camp food, and added, "Please tell Lucy that I miss her strawberry shortcake almost as much as I miss you."

"Lucy is the girl who works in the house," I said. "She must have been . . . must be . . . Prudence's maid, or something."

"She looks pretty good for being more than eighty years old," said Simon.

The next few letters were all very short. Henry seemed to be spending a lot of time learning how to shoot a rifle and dig holes to hide in. By the end of the day, he was too tired to do anything but write Prudence quick notes saying how much he missed her.

"This isn't telling us anything," said Simon.

"Be patient," I said. "We have some more to go through."

But Simon was right. Almost all of Henry's letters to Prudence were filled with nothing more than "I miss yous" and "until we see each other agains." They might have been romantic, but they weren't getting us any closer to solving the mystery of the snow globe.

Eventually, there were only three unopened letters left. I opened the first of the three.

October 28, 1917

Dearest Prudence:

Well, we have had only the most basic of training, but we are needed across the sea as soon as possible. The boys are planning a big push against the opposition in France and our numbers are needed, if only as reinforcement.

I confess that there is a little bit of trepidation in my heart as I think about what might lie ahead. But I am willing to do what I must, and the thought of you waiting at home for me will keep me strong and bring me back again. Please remember me and

*the rest of our troops in your prayers. If all goes
well, I will be back in your arms before spring.*

*We leave tomorrow, and I do not know when I
will get another chance to write to you. If you do
not hear from me, know that I think of you every
moment of every day.*

>*With all my love,
Henry*

"Wow, they must have shipped him out right away,"
said Simon. "I wonder where he ended up."
I opened the second-to-last letter and unfolded it. Unlike
the other ones, this one was written on a piece of paper that
seemed to have been torn from something else. The handwriting was shaky, as though it had been written very
quickly, and there were some stains on it that looked like
dirt.

November 19, 1917

Dearest Prudence:

*I am sorry to be so long in writing to you. You
must think that something terrible has befallen me.*

*In actuality, I am in a field camp in the country-
side of France. I cannot tell you exactly where, in*

case this letter ends up in enemy hands, but also because I really do not know where I am. I know only that there is fighting nearby. At night I hear the sounds of gunfire and smell smoke in the air. At daylight the wounded are brought in to the makeshift hospital we have set up.

Despite this, I cannot help but say that the small town nearby is very lovely. I wish that you could see the beautiful old houses and hear the voices of the women as they chatter while doing their wash in the creek. Someday when this war is over I should like to come back here with you and see it again in all its beauty.

Please excuse my terrible handwriting. I am attempting to write in haste on the back of a notice that was tacked up in town. A friend is leaving in only minutes to return to Paris, and he will mail this for me.

Here he is now. I must sign off, and leave you with the words . . .

> *I love you,*
> *Henry*

I turned the letter over. Sure enough, he had written the letter on the back of some kind of flyer. It was torn in half, so I couldn't see the whole thing, but I could make out a picture of what looked like a German soldier. He looked angry, and underneath the picture there were words written in French.

"Now I wish I'd paid more attention in Mr. Flagel's French class," I said. "I'd love to know what this says."

"Probably something about not taking candy from strangers," said Simon.

"I wouldn't take anything from that guy," I said. "What a creep."

I folded up the letter and put it back. There was only one more to read. I hoped it would give us the next clue we needed. So far, we'd learned a lot about Henry, but it wasn't really getting us anywhere. I took a deep breath and opened up the final letter.

December 1, 1917

Dearest Prudence:

It seems strange to be sending you Christmas greetings so early in the month, but who knows when you will get this, if ever. The fighting here has advanced quickly, and I do not know how much of our mail is actually getting through and back to our loved ones in America. The last letter from you arrived here two weeks ago, and I have heard noth-

ing since. I can only assume that the letters have been lost.

How I wish that I could be with you during the upcoming holidays. I remember as though it were yesterday the way you smiled as we danced at your Christmas Eve party last year. Your eyes sparkled so, and your laughter filled the room even more than the music we danced to. Promise me that you will dance for me this Christmas Eve as well, so that I may think of you as I keep watch under the cold night skies of France and know that the same stars that shine upon me shine also upon you.

I know it is foolish to attempt this, but I am sending you a small gift. I doubt that it will ever reach your hands, but I have to try. There is in the village here a man who makes the most amazing things—glass globes filled with water and containing miniature scenes. Most of his creations depict scenes from the countryside. But I have told him stories of Shady Corners at Christmastime and described for him your house, and he has fashioned it in miniature, right down to the weather vane on the roof of the house. It is the most exquisite little thing I have ever seen, and I know it will delight you.

I wish I were bringing this gift to you myself, to place in your hands with my own. But that time will have to wait. For now, I send it in care of another and pray that it arrives safely. If it does reach you, please gaze into it and imagine me running up the steps to greet you as the carolers sing to us of the joys of Christmas. How I long for that day to come.

Merry Christmas, my love.
Henry

When I finished the letter, I folded it neatly and slipped it back into the envelope. Then I picked up the snow globe and looked into it.

"It's hard to imagine that it came all the way from France," I said. "How did it make it without breaking?"

"And what happened to Henry, and what does all of this have to do with December twenty-fourth?" said Simon.

I put the globe down again. I took the letters and retied them with the lavender ribbon. Prudence had kept them carefully all those years, and there had to be a good reason why. There also had to be a good reason for her appearing now in Eerie. Then I remembered the painting hanging on the landing of Prudence's house. It was a picture of Henry in his army uniform.

"We have to get into that house," I said after I told

Simon about the painting. "Everything we need to know to solve this mystery is in there."

"Yeah, but Lucy always stops us," he said. "How are we going to get past her?"

I stood up and started for the door. "I'm not sure yet," I said as we left the Secret Spot. "We'll have to figure it out as we go along."

7

*O*nce again we found ourselves outside in the snow. By now I was getting a little tired of the winter wonderland that was Eerie. I mean, I'm all for snow, but this storm seemed like it was never going to end. The path my father had shoveled that morning was already gone, and most people had simply stopped trying to dig themselves out.

The only person who seemed not to mind the snow was Mr. Stamps, the mailman. He was walking down the street with his bag slung over his shoulder as usual, his blue hat pulled down over his eyes to keep the snow out. He just plowed through the drifting snow like a ship through water.

"Hey, Mr. Stamps," I said. "You're certainly dedicated to your job to be out in this weather."

"Well, this is our busiest day of the year," he said. "Everyone's sending Christmas cards at the last minute. Someone's got to make sure they get delivered. Besides, you know our motto: 'Neither sleet nor snow nor freezing rain shall keep the postman from his appointed rounds.' ''

"I always thought that was a joke," said Simon, "sort of like 'teacher knows best.' ''

Mr. Stamps frowned. "The postal service is no laughing matter, young man. We take our duties seriously. Very seriously."

"I'm sure you do," I said. "So we better let you get back to work, then. Merry Christmas."

"Yeah, Merry Christmas," said Simon.

"It will be," said Mr. Stamps. "Thanks to me." He went to the next mailbox and stuck a bundle of letters in it. Then he continued on down the street, his bag brushing snow from the bushes as he passed.

"Imagine having to deliver Christmas cards every day for the rest of your life," I said. "You'd never have a day off."

"I don't think he'd notice," said Simon. "He loves the mail."

We'd come to the corner of Mulder and Scully. Prudence Lively's house was still there. Smoke was pouring in a thin stream from the chimney, and I could see lights on downstairs. I could also see shadows moving behind the curtains, as though someone were busy running around.

"I wonder what's going on in there," said Simon.

"Let's stand here and wait," I suggested. "Maybe we'll find out."

A few minutes later the front door opened. Lucy ran out, pulling her coat on as she closed the door. She turned and ran down the steps, her cheeks flushed with color.

"Excuse me," she said when she saw us. "Do you know where I might find chestnuts?"

"Chestnuts?" said Simon.

Lucy nodded. If she remembered seeing us before, she showed no sign of it. She also seemed to have forgotten all about the tragedy she spoke of the night before. "Yes," she said. "I need to get them for the party. The guests will be here in four hours, and I completely forgot about the roasted chestnuts. They're Miss's favorite. If we don't have them, she will be so disappointed."

I thought for a minute. "The Greens House might have them," I said. "That's the produce store on Main Street."

Lucy smiled. "Thank you so much," she said. "This will make Miss so happy tonight."

She started to run down the street, but turned around. "Merry Christmas," she said.

"Same to you," I said, and she took off in search of her chestnuts.

"That was weird," said Simon when Lucy was gone. "What was all that talk about a party? There was certainly no party going on last night when we caroled here. In fact, the place looked like a funeral parlor."

"We're missing something," I said. "Some big piece of the puzzle that will make it all start to make sense."

"I wonder what she's doing in there," said Simon. "I wish we could see through the windows."

We walked up the steps to the front door and knelt in the snow. There was a thin mail slot built into the bottom of the door. Simon lifted the brass flap and peered inside.

"What do you see?" I asked.

"Not much," he said. "I can see a piece of a pine garland on the banister . . . but that's about it."

"Do you see her?"

Simon shook his head. "No, but I can hear her singing somewhere. She's humming a song—it's really pretty. She sounds happy."

"Not at all like last night," I said. "Something must have happened. Something awful. But what was it? And why isn't she sad anymore?"

As I was thinking, someone came walking up the steps. I jumped, thinking that it was Lucy coming back from buying the chestnuts. I didn't want her to catch us spying on Prudence. But it wasn't her. It was a man in a brown uniform.

"This where one Prudence Lively lives?" he said, looking at a clipboard in his hand.

"Um, yes," I said. "This is her house."

"Got a package for her then," said the man. He held out the clipboard and a pen. "Just sign right there."

"But I'm not her," I said.

"You live here?" he asked impatiently.

I started to say no, but then I thought of something. "Yes," I said instead. "I live here. I'm Miss Lively's nephew."

"Good enough for me," the man said. "I got a truck full of packages that need to be out by five. Can't be waiting around for signatures all day."

I signed the clipboard, and he handed me a small box wrapped in white paper and sealed with lots of tape. Then he got back into his truck and drove away, his tires spinning in the snow as he went.

I looked down at the package in my hand. It felt heavy. And there was a letter attached to it. The address was written in the same handwriting as on the letters we'd read.

"It's from him," I said to Simon. "It's from Henry. And I bet anything I know what's inside this box."

"The snow globe," said Simon. "Are you going to open it?"

"No," I said. "I don't think that would be right. Whatever happens to this box has to happen for us to figure out what's going on."

"So what are you going to do, then?"

I looked up at the front door. "I'm going to deliver it," I said. I pulled the bell cord. I heard the jingling of a bell inside, then a voice as Prudence ran to the door.

"Coming," she said happily. "Is that you, Lucy?"

She threw open the door.

"Oh," she said when she saw me. "I thought you were Lucy, my maid."

"No, ma'am," I said. "I have a delivery for you." I was staring at her face. She looked so pretty, so happy. Not at all like the sad woman in black I'd seen sitting in the audience at the pageant the night before. She looked just like she did in the photos I had of her.

"A delivery?" she said. "For me? I wonder what on earth it could be."

I held out the package, and she took it in her hands. When she saw the handwriting on the paper, she smiled.

"Oh, my," she said. "It's from Henry." She turned to me. "My fiancé," she explained. "He's away in France fighting in the war."

I nodded. I didn't know what to say. I wanted her to open the box so I could see if it really was the snow globe. But she just kept holding it in her hands. Finally, she noticed me watching her.

"I'm so sorry," she said. "You're waiting for your tip. Let me see what I have in my pocket."

"Oh, no," I said. "No. That's quite all right. I was just . . . um . . . admiring your home. It's very lovely."

She smiled again. "Why, thank you," she said. "We're getting ready for a Christmas Eve party. It's going to be wonderful. Dancing . . . Music . . . Food . . . I only wish that Henry could be here to see it. He loves parties."

She looked at the box again. "But this makes everything just perfect. Thank you so much for delivering it. It was very kind of you to come out in this snow."

"Don't mention it," I said, thinking of Mr. Stamps. "After all, it is my job. Have a Merry Christmas."

"Merry Christmas to you, too," she said. "You've just made mine the happiest one ever."

She closed the door, and I heard the sounds of her tearing the tape off of the package. Unable to resist, I knelt down and peered through the mail slot. Simon ran up and knelt next to me.

"What's she doing?" he said. "Is she opening it?"

"There's a lot of tape," I said. "She got a letter opener, and she's sitting in the hallway, cutting it all off."

Prudence took the letter off the package first, slicing it open with the letter opener and pulling the paper out. She read it quickly, her eyes scanning the page and her lips moving slightly as she read Henry's words. I felt strange watching her read a letter I knew was sitting up on my desk, especially when I knew what it said before she did.

I could see Prudence gasp as she read the last part of the letter.

"I think she just read the part about the snow globe," I whispered to Simon.

Sure enough, Prudence put the letter down on a small table in the hallway and started to pull the paper off of the package. Now that the tape had been cut, the paper peeled away easily. Prudence dropped it to the floor. Then she pulled the top off of the box and started to pull out more crumpled-up paper. Finally, she lifted the snow globe out and held it in her hands.

I saw tears form in her eyes as she looked at the little village inside the glass ball. Twice she brought her fingertips to her mouth, as though she were about to cry. Then she gave the globe a little shake. When she saw the snow billow up, she let out a little shriek of glee.

"It's the same snow globe, all right," I said to Simon. "Even from this far away I can tell."

Prudence was kneeling in the hallway, holding the snow globe up to her face and shaking it repeatedly, squealing with delight like a small girl each time she saw the snowstorm contained inside the glass and water.

"Uh-oh," said Simon, tugging on my sleeve. "We'd better hide. Lucy's coming back."

I looked over my shoulder and saw Lucy. She had just turned the corner, and she hadn't seen us yet. We stood up and hurried down the steps, hiding around the corner of the house where she couldn't see us. I peeked around the corner and watched as she went up the steps and into the house. She was carrying a small paper bag, so I assumed she'd found her chestnuts.

A minute or so after Lucy closed the door, we heard laughter coming from inside.

"Prudence must be showing her the snow globe," I said.

There was another series of giggles.

"Prudence seems really happy," said Simon. "She got Henry's letter and the gift. What could possibly make her so sad later in the evening? I mean, why would Lucy say there had been a great tragedy if everything worked out okay?"

"Maybe the present makes her miss Henry," I suggested. "Or maybe nobody shows up for the party."

"That doesn't seem like a big enough tragedy to make someone live the same day over and over again," Simon said. "Something else must happen."

"Yeah, but what?" I said. "We can't just keep standing around out here."

Before we could decide what to do next, someone else came walking down the street. It was another man, only this one was wearing a soldier's uniform.

"It's Henry!" said Simon.

But it wasn't. The man looked a little like Henry, but he was shorter and heavier, and he had light hair. He looked sad, and when he reached Prudence's house, he looked back and forth from the number on the door to a piece of paper in his hands several times before taking a deep breath and going up the steps. He pulled the bell cord and waited, his hands held anxiously behind his back, until Lucy opened the door.

"Can I help you?" she asked.

"Are you Miss Prudence Lively?" the man asked.

Lucy shook her head. "No, just one moment, please."

A few seconds later, Prudence appeared at the door. She was still smiling. "Hello," she said. "Can I help you?"

The man cleared his throat. "I'm with the army, ma'am," the man said. "I've been sent to bring you news about your fiancé, Henry Collins."

"Henry?" said Prudence. Then her face lit up. "Is he coming home?" she said. "Is my Henry coming back? Oh, that would be the greatest Christmas gift I could ever receive."

The man shook his head. "No, ma'am, I'm afraid it's not that."

Prudence stopped smiling. "What is it?" she said. "What's happened?"

"I hate to have to tell you this," he said. "Especially being that it's Christmas Eve and all. But I've been sent to inform you that Private Henry Collins was killed in the line of duty on the twenty-second day of December."

8

*A*ll of the color drained from Prudence's face. She grabbed the door frame for support, as though she were about to collapse. The man reached out to help her, but she waved his hand away.

"Dead," she said, her voice barely a whisper. "That can't be. There must be some mistake. Henry can't be dead. I just received a letter and gift from him. See?"

She held out the letter as though it were proof that what the soldier said was a lie. Her eyes filled with tears as she looked at the man's face, waiting for him to tell her that he had the wrong house, or the wrong Henry Collins.

"No, ma'am, there's no mistake," the man said. "Private Collins was killed fighting the Germans. It's right here in this letter."

He handed Prudence a letter. She opened it and read it. When she was done, she crumpled it up in her fist and began to cry. The man looked at her, not knowing what to say. Finally he said, "You should be proud of him, ma'am. I'm just sorry it had to turn out this way. Really sorry.''

Prudence was crying heavily. Lucy came to the door and put an arm around her.

''Come inside,'' she said gently.

She drew Prudence into the house and shut the door. The man looked at the closed door and turned around. Very slowly, he walked down the steps and started back down the street. Part of me wanted to follow him, to see where he went when he turned the corner, but I was rooted to the spot. I couldn't believe what had just happened.

''I guess now we know what the tragedy is,'' said Simon.

''What a horrible story,'' I said. ''And it happened on Christmas Eve. No wonder she doesn't want anyone to see her tonight.''

''It still doesn't explain the blizzard or the fact that she keeps living this one day over and over,'' said Simon.

''Or why I saw her sitting in the audience during the pageant,'' I said. ''There's still more to this story.''

''But to find out what it is, we have to be in there, I bet,'' said Simon, nodding toward the house.

''That's right,'' I answered.

''And just how will we do that?''

''Well, if tonight goes like last night did, Mrs. Marlowe will be coming around with her carolers again. If we're with them, I think this time we can get inside."

Simon moaned. "Not more singing," he said. "I thought I'd sung my last carol last night."

"If we play our cards right," I said, "this will be the last time. Come on, we have to get ready."

We left Prudence and Lucy crying behind the closed front door and went back to my house. Up in my room, I picked up the snow globe and looked at it. I imagined Prudence a few blocks away, holding the same snow globe in her hands and crying. Somehow our lives had crossed, and the snow globe was responsible for it. I put the globe down and looked at the photographs. Henry was dead, and Prudence was reliving the day she found out, taking the rest of us along with her in the process. I knew that Simon and I were the ones who were supposed to bring an end to it, but I didn't know how we would do it.

"The pageant should be getting started soon," I said, looking at my watch.

"I wonder how Mrs. Marlowe is getting along without us," said Simon. "Who do you think she roped into playing the shepherds?"

"I don't know," I said. "I'm just glad it isn't us."

Outside my window the storm had picked up again, and the snow was blowing against the glass.

"This is just what happened last night," said Simon. "I wonder why it gets worse the later it gets."

"Just make sure you dress warm tonight," I said. "I don't know how long we'll have to stay out in this. It could be a while."

"That's okay," said Simon. "Last night my mother made me wear the nightshirt my aunt Esther made me. I wouldn't mind missing that, especially since I know she'll have totally forgotten the whole evening by tomorrow morning."

"Yeah," I said. "I'd be happy to skip stringing lights myself. Once a year is more than enough."

As the time neared for the caroling to start, we bundled up again and left the house. Just like the previous night, the wind whipped at our scarves, trying to pull them from around our necks as we made our way to World of Stuff. By the time we got there, my skin was red and I was freezing.

"It seems even worse tonight," I said to Simon as we pushed open the door.

Inside, the carolers were just warming up. When Mrs. Marlowe saw us, she waved.

"Hello, boys," she said. "You just missed the most wonderful pageant. I tried to talk to you two earlier, but you got away from me."

I laughed nervously. "We must not have seen you," I said.

She patted me on the shoulder. "That's okay. Actually, things went splendidly. I asked the King and Mayor Chisel to play the shepherds. They were a smashing success. You should have heard the King singing. People were fainting in the aisles. I've never seen anything like it."

"I can imagine," I said. I wondered if Prudence had been there, but I didn't dare ask.

Simon and I joined the group of carolers and went through the rehearsal. Mrs. Marlowe sang all the same songs as the night before, so I felt as though I'd already practiced them once. When she was satisfied that we all knew our parts, we started off.

I was anxious to get to Prudence's house, and I tried to hurry the group along. As soon as we finished a song, I'd start to walk to the next house. "Come on," I said cheerfully. "We don't want anyone to miss out." The other carolers seemed to agree, and before long we were back in front of Prudence's house.

"What shall we sing here?" said Mrs. Marlowe. "Does anyone have any suggestions?"

"How about 'Frosty the Snowman'?" said Mr. Radford. "I love that one."

"I have a better idea," I said before everyone could start singing.

"What's that, Marshall?" said Mrs. Marlowe.

"I . . . um . . . I think Simon should sing a solo."

"You do?" said Mrs. Marlowe.

"You *what?*" said Simon, staring at me open-mouthed.

"Yeah," I said. "Simon has a great voice. I think

everyone should hear him, and what better time than now?''

"I think that's a wonderful idea," said Mrs. Marlowe. "What would he like to sing?"

"Yeah," said Simon. "What would I like to sing, Marshall?"

I thought for a minute. "How about 'Silent Night'?" I said. "That's an old favorite."

"Good idea," said Mrs. Marlowe. "Simon, you stand right up front here, so everyone can hear you." She grabbed Simon's hand and pulled him out of the group. He tried to get away, but she had a firm grip on him.

"Now, you just stand here," she said. "I want to hear that beautiful voice of yours."

Simon looked at me, scowling. I knew he was mad, but I had an idea. "Go on," I mouthed at him. "Sing."

Simon opened his mouth. "Silent night," he began, his voice soft and shaking.

Everyone was watching Simon sing, so they didn't notice when I went up the steps and stood beside the front door. I was sort of in the shadows, and with all the snow falling, I blended in pretty well. Only Simon had seen me go up the steps, and he knew what I had in mind.

Down on the sidewalk, Simon kept singing. "Holy night," he sang, a little more loudly. "All is calm, all is bright."

He was getting louder with each line, and the louder

he got, the more everyone listened. He sounded terrible. His voice cracked and he was off-key.

"Sleep in heavenly pee—eace!" he wailed. "Sle—eep in heavenly peace."

Just as he reached the high point of the song, the front door flew open. It was Lucy. She stepped outside and looked at the crowd on the sidewalk.

"What on earth is all this racket?" she demanded. "It sounds like someone being murdered out here!"

As she moved away from the door, I quietly slipped behind her and inside the house. She was so busy looking at Simon that she didn't even notice me as I moved quickly into the front hall and then through a doorway. A moment later, I heard her shut the door again.

"Honestly," she said. "Some people have no respect for the privacy of others. And that poor child. He sounds positively ill. It's a good thing Miss isn't home yet or she would have been sick with grief."

I heard her go up the stairs. When I was sure she was gone, I ran back to the front door and opened it. As I'd expected, Simon was huddled on the steps.

"Get in here," I said quietly.

He came inside, and I shut the door again, making sure not to make any noise. I motioned for Simon to follow me into the other room.

"I am going to get you for that," he said. "I am going to get you so bad you will never forget it. What was the big idea?"

"I had to make a distraction," I said, defending myself.

"Fine, but next time, *you* get to be the distraction," he said. "That was the most humiliating experience of my entire life."

"Don't worry," I said. "Tomorrow it will be like it never happened at all."

"Well, *I'll* remember it," he said. "And what are we doing in here, anyway?"

"Getting some answers," I said. "I heard Lucy say something about Prudence not being home yet. She must not have come back from the pageant. That gives us a little time to look around."

I peered back into the front hall. There was no sign of Lucy. I started for the stairs. I wanted to get a good look at the painting on the landing.

Stepping carefully on the stairs in case they creaked, I went up them with Simon right behind me. We made it to the landing with no problem and stopped in front of the picture.

"That's Henry, all right," Simon said. "He looks just like he did in that photo."

In the painting, Henry was looking out from the canvas with a sadness in his eyes. He was wearing the same brown uniform, and sticking out of the front pocket of his shirt was the top of a picture. It was the picture of Prudence.

"She must have had it done after he went into the

army," I said. "They must have really loved each other."

"True love never dies," said a voice on the stairs above us. Simon and I both jumped about a foot and turned around. Lucy was standing on the second floor, looking down at us. She didn't look angry or even surprised. She was just watching us.

"We were just . . ." I started to say, desperately trying to think of some reasonable excuse to explain why we were standing on the landing of a house we had no business being in.

"You were just looking," said Lucy. "I know what you're doing. I remember you from last night."

"You do?" said Simon. "But this morning when you saw us you pretended not to know who we were."

"I had to be sure," said Lucy.

"Sure of what?" I asked.

"Sure that you knew."

"Knew what?" I said.

Lucy paused for a moment before going on. "About the curse," she said. "I had to be sure that you remembered what happened yesterday."

"Oh, we remember, all right," I said. "I don't think we'll ever forget it."

"So you know what's going on here?" said Simon.

Lucy smiled. She seemed sad. "Oh, yes," she said. "It has been going on for a very long time, as you probably guessed. You are the first ones to arrive who also know about it.''

"You mean about it always being the same day?'' I said.

Lucy nodded. "In this house, it will always be December the twenty-fourth, nineteen seventeen. There have been others who have come before you, of course, but none of them ever figured it out. They came here by accident.''

"And what happened to them?'' asked Simon, as though he didn't really want to know the answer.

"They remained here,'' said Lucy. "In this time. Or, more precisely, in the in-between time. This house is caught between the hours, neither here nor there.''

"Forever?'' Simon said.

"Forever,'' said Lucy. "Or until the curse is broken. But no one knows how to do that.''

"Are you the only other one who knows what's going on?'' I asked.

Lucy nodded her head. "The others forget while they sleep. They wake up thinking it is a new day. But I never forget.''

"I don't understand,'' I said. "At least not completely. I know that it's always the same day. And I know that Mr. Collins is dead. But who put the curse on the house?''

Lucy came down the stairs and stopped in front of

the painting. She looked up at Henry Collins' painted face. Then she looked into mine.

"Why, Miss Lively did," she said.

9

"**M**iss Lively put the curse on *herself?*" I said in disbelief.

"I know it sounds strange," said Lucy. "And I suppose it is. But yes, she's responsible for what is going on here, even though she has no memory of it."

"I don't get it," said Simon. "Why would she curse herself?"

"Like I said earlier," said Lucy. "For true love."

She looked up at the painting of Henry Collins again. "They loved one another like no other people I've known," said Lucy. "When she found out that he had died, her heart was broken."

"But what about the curse?" I said. "How did that happen?"

"After she heard about Henry, Miss Lively was determined that Christmas should go on as planned," explained Lucy. "We were all set to have a grand party. The guests were invited, the food was ready, the house was decorated."

"Just like it is now," I said, and Lucy nodded.

"Miss Lively knew that Henry would have loved the party," she explained. "She thought that if we held it as planned that somehow it would make her feel better."

"So what happened?" asked Simon.

"Miss Lively had planned on attending a Christmas Eve pageant put on by the local children," said Lucy. "It was a tradition in Shady Corners."

"That explains why Mrs. Marlowe needed us," I said.

"She went to the pageant," said Lucy. "But watching it made her sadder than ever. She rushed home afterwards, and when she got here, she went into a fury. She ripped the garlands from the walls, broke the decorations, and cried until she was hysterical. There was nothing I could do to calm her."

"Is that why the house was dark when we came caroling last night?" I asked.

"She had just collapsed and been put to bed," explained Lucy. "Tonight you came early. She has not yet arrived home, but she should be here any moment."

"But the *curse*," said Simon. "Get to the curse."

"That night, Miss Lively sat up in her room, holding the snow globe that Mr. Collins sent her in her hands. Several times I went by to check on her, and each time she was sitting in the chair by the window, her eyes fixed on the globe. The last time I walked by, I heard her talking."

"What was she saying?" Simon urged. I thought he was going to burst from the excitement.

"It was the curse," said Lucy. "Although at the time I didn't know that. How could I? She was staring into the globe and holding Mr. Collins' picture to her heart. I will never forget her words. She said, 'I cannot face Christmas morning without my beloved. I wish that this night would never end, that the snow would storm and blow forever until we are together once more.' Then she shook the snow globe, and the tiny village inside was covered up by the snow."

"That's not much of a curse," said Simon. "I mean, it's not like she said someone would die on her eighteenth birthday or something."

"It was enough," said Lucy. "As I said, I thought nothing of it at first. I thought they were just the words of a grieving woman. I went back downstairs and tidied up the house for the morning. Then I went to bed. When I awoke the next day, I rose and went to prepare breakfast."

"Let me guess," I said. "There had been a terrible snowstorm."

"That's right. The entire town was covered in it. I'd never seen such a thing. But even more surprising was Miss Lively. When I went to bring her a breakfast tray, she met me on the stairs, as happy as could be. She acted as though nothing were wrong at all. 'Isn't the snow delightful, Lucy?' she said to me. And when I answered, 'Yes, it makes for a very merry Christmas morning,' she laughed. 'You're too excited about the party,' she said. 'You've jumped a day ahead.' ''

"That's just what happened to me!" I said. "My father thought I was crazy."

"Well, at first I thought *she* was crazy," said Lucy. "I thought that maybe she'd had amnesia or something after the shock of the day before. But I said nothing. Then, when I went to fetch the morning paper and saw the date on it, I thought that *I* was the lunatic. I convinced myself that I'd dreamed everything that had occurred—the package, the soldier, the news of Mr. Collins' death. Watching Miss Lively going about the day so full of joy, I couldn't possibly believe that any of it had really happened."

"When did you figure it out?" I asked.

"When the bell rang after noon and the man was there with the package again. I opened the door expecting the boy from the market with the oysters I'd ordered, but instead there was the very same man I was sure I must have dreamed up. I was so startled I dropped the pitcher I was carrying and it shattered. I felt as though I'd seen a ghost."

"Well, we certainly know what *that's* like," said Simon.

"What?" said Lucy, looking confused.

"It's a long story," I said. "We'll save it for another

time. Let's just say that Simon and I are used to seeing weird stuff. It's actually pretty normal for us.''

"Well, it wasn't normal for me," said Lucy. "I didn't know what to do. I just kept staring at the man until finally he asked me if I was all right. I wasn't all right at all, but I took the package from him and gave it to Miss Lively. I watched as she opened it and took out the same snow globe she'd opened the day before. I listened to her exclaim over Henry's letter in exactly the same words she'd used twenty-four hours before.''

"Did you know yet what was happening?" I asked.

"No, I still thought I had dreamed it, or was dreaming it. I kept waiting to wake up. But I didn't. Then, when the soldier came a while later telling us that Henry was dead all over again, I remembered Miss Lively's words of the night before. I couldn't believe that what she'd wished for had come true. I prayed that I was wrong. It was too horrible to imagine. But then the dawn came again, and again it was the twenty-fourth of December, and I knew it was all too true.''

"And Miss Lively has no idea what she's done?" said Simon.

"None at all," said Lucy. "Each morning she wakes up thinking that it will be a happy day. And each night she curses this house and everyone in it.''

"Have you ever tried to break the curse?" I asked.

"The third day, I tried," said Lucy. "I went into Miss Lively's bedroom and smashed the snow globe. I threw it to the floor as hard as I could, and watched as it shattered into pieces and the water ran out across the carpet. I thought that would end it.''

''But apparently it didn't,'' I said.

''No, the next day was the same as the one before it,'' said Lucy. ''And it's been that way ever since. Never Christmas. Always Christmas Eve.''

''Well,'' I said. ''I think it's about time we ended this curse. I for one don't want to spend forever trapped in December the twenty-fourth.''

Before we could continue our conversation, there was the sound of a key turning in the front door.

''It's Miss Lively!'' said Lucy. ''Quick, you must hide. She cannot see you here.''

Lucy dashed up the stairs to the second floor, with Simon and me right behind her. She pushed us toward a door.

''Hide in there,'' she said. ''Don't make a noise. And whatever you do, don't come out until I come for you.''

We ran into the room and Lucy slammed the door shut behind us. It was a guest bedroom. I heard Lucy running back down the stairs. I heard the front door close, and then I heard Prudence Lively's voice.

''I can't do it, Lucy,'' she said, and began to sob. ''I cannot have the party tonight. I tried, I really did. I went to the pageant, just like Henry would have wanted me to. But without him beside me . . . ''

Her voice was choked off by the sounds of crying.

Lucy said something to Prudence that I couldn't hear. Then there was more weeping. This was followed by a crash, like someone had thrown something onto the floor.

"Take it down, Lucy," wailed Miss Lively. "Take it all down. I don't want to see any of it. No reminders of this cursed holiday. Take it down. Burn it. Burn it all. I want to see it go up in smoke."

There was no more talking, but I could hear the sounds of the garlands being pulled down from around the banisters, and the muffled crashes of ornaments being broken. But most of all I could hear Prudence Lively crying.

"She must be ripping the place apart," said Simon. "It sounds horrible."

It *did* sound horrible. Every few seconds there was another crash, and I could only imagine what the floor looked like strewn with the bits and pieces of Christmas. I was glad that we were upstairs where we couldn't see it. I felt bad for Prudence, but I felt worse for Lucy. She had to live through this every day, while everyone else forgot about it in their sleep. And now that we knew the secret of the snow globe, we would have to live through it every day, too. I had to think of a way to help her—to help all of us.

Prudence was talking again. She was walking up the stairs, sobbing and calling out to Lucy.

"Cancel the party tonight," she said, her voice

trembling. "I can't face any guests. I need to be alone. I can't bear to hear music or laughing. I can't bear it at all. Send them all away."

"Yes, ma'am," Lucy said in a tired voice. "I'm sure they'll understand. I'll bring you up a tray later."

"No food," Prudence said. "Nothing for me. I wish to be left in peace."

"Yes, ma'am," Lucy answered.

I heard Lucy go back down the stairs, but Prudence continued on down the hall. She was almost directly outside our door, and I could hear everything clearly through the walls. She was sobbing again, her cries muffled but still loud.

"Oh, Henry," she said. "What shall I do without you? What shall I do? I shall never be happy again."

She cried for a few more minutes, her sobs growing more and more terrible to hear. Then she continued on down the hall. I heard her walking up the stairs to the third floor, and then everything was quiet.

A minute later Lucy was at the door, unlocking it. "Come downstairs," she said. "Miss Lively will be up there for the rest of the night, but you need to leave quickly."

We followed Lucy out into the hall and down the stairs. When I saw the mess, I gasped. Every pine garland had been torn into pieces, and the hallway was littered with pieces of broken glass. Dishes had been smashed, and even the mirror was broken into hundreds of tiny shards.

"It looks like a bomb went off in here," I said.

"It's like this every night," said Lucy. "It will take me most of the night to clean it up."

"And then tomorrow you get to do it all again," said Simon. "That *is* some curse."

"How I wish there was a way to end it," said Lucy sadly.

I looked around the hallway at the destruction caused by Prudence Lively's grief. I thought about the food sitting in the kitchen and the tree waiting in the parlor to be trimmed. I thought about the box of ornaments sitting on the floor at the back of World of Stuff.

"Maybe there is a way to end it," I said.

Simon and Lucy looked at me.

"How?" said Lucy. "What could bring an end to this and make things right again?"

I grinned. "We're going to have a party," I said.

10

"A party?" said Simon incredulously. "How can we have a party at a time like this?"

"A *Christmas* party," I said.

Lucy and Simon looked at each other. I could tell they thought I'd gone crazy, and weren't sure what they should do.

"Don't you see?" I said. "Prudence cancels the party because she's upset. Then she goes upstairs and sits in her room all night, getting sadder and sadder about Henry's death. That's when she makes the wish on the snow globe and brings the curse on the house."

Lucy was nodding now. "That's right," she said. "It's because she doesn't have the party to take her mind off things that she becomes so despondent."

Now Simon was getting the picture. "So if she goes through with the party . . . " he said.

"Then she doesn't make the wish," we all finished together.

"Right," I said. "So what we have to do is make

sure that the party goes on as planned. Then maybe the curse will be broken.''

''Maybe?'' said Simon.

I shrugged. ''Well, we can't be sure until we try it,'' I said. ''I don't have any better ideas, do you?''

''I guess not,'' he said. ''But how are we going to pull this off?''

''Tomorrow will be the twenty-fourth all over again,'' I said. ''Prudence will wake up like she always does, thinking that she's going to have a Christmas Eve party. You and I will come over and help Lucy get things ready.''

''I can tell her that you're the boys I hired for the day,'' Lucy said.

''Good idea. We'll go get the box of old ornaments from World of Stuff. Then we'll make this place sparkle.''

''What about the snow globe and the soldier with the letter about Henry?'' said Lucy.

''We'll take care of that tomorrow,'' I said. ''Right now we have a party to plan.''

Lucy got a piece of paper and began to write out all of the things we would need for the party the next day. Since she'd planned the same party every day for eighty years, she knew exactly what we had to get.

''I'll make the food,'' she said. ''But you'll need to get a Christmas tree and garlands for the banisters.''

''That's easy enough,'' I said. ''Mr. Tannenbaum

sells trees in town. We'll get a big one there. It will be the best tree you've ever seen."

We went over the rest of the list. Then Simon and I left Lucy and went home. The storm was raging, and I knew that Prudence was up in her room looking out her window and wishing that the storm would erase the whole world. I remembered how she had sounded, sobbing in the hallway, and I hoped more than anything that we would be able to pull off the party the next night. If it didn't work, I didn't have another plan.

When I got back to my house, my dad was stringing lights on the tree again. Just like before, they were wrapped around his legs. I sighed and went in to help him.

The rest of that Christmas Eve went exactly as it had the first time. I managed to go through the motions, pretending to be all excited, but I was relieved when it was time to go to bed. As I closed my eyes, I half hoped that when I woke up it would really be Christmas, and everything that had happened that day would be a dream. But another part of me hoped it wouldn't. That part wanted to see what was going to happen. And in the end, that part of me was bigger than the other part.

I woke up the next morning feeling excited and scared. I knew it would either be the last day of the curse or another day of an eternity spent caught in the in-between time. What made it worse was that only Simon, Lucy, and I knew about it. Everyone else in

Eerie thought it was just another Christmas Eve. I knew that downstairs, my mother was fixing breakfast and my father was looking at the paper, commenting on how no one made good movies anymore. Syndi was probably washing her hair and thinking about what she was going to wear. And I was lying in my bed watching the snow come down and thinking about breaking an eighty-year-old curse. Now I knew how those fairy godmothers in *Sleeping Beauty* must have felt.

Finally I dragged myself out of bed and got dressed. I went downstairs, wolfed down some toast and orange juice, and told my parents I was going out to do my paper route. Then I ran over to Simon's house. He met me at the door.

"Ready?" I said.

"Ready as I'll ever be," he answered. "Let's go get that tree."

We walked into town and went to Mr. Tannenbaum's tree stand.

"Good morning," he said. "You boys looking for a Christmas tree today?"

"We sure are," I said. "The biggest one you've got."

Mr. Tannenbaum led us through the rows and rows of trees, each one tied up neatly with twine. He stopped in front of the biggest tree I'd ever seen. It had to be at least nine feet tall, and it was a beautiful bluish color.

"Here you go," he said. "The best tree on the lot. A blue spruce. Don't get many of them."

"It's perfect," I said. "We'll take it."

Mr. Tannenbaum bundled up the tree with a rope.

"That should do it," he said, pulling the collar of his coat tighter around him. "I hope this storm lets up soon. This should be my busiest day of the year."

"I hear it might be ending tonight," I said. I hoped it was true.

We walked back down the street, dragging the tree behind us. When we got to World of Stuff, Simon waited outside while I ran in. Mr. Radford was behind the counter, humming to himself and cutting snowflakes out of white paper.

"Good morning, Mr. Radford," I said.

"Ah, Marshall," he said. "What can I do for you?"

"Well, I was hoping you could do me a favor," I said. "You have a box of old Christmas ornaments back there. I was wondering if I could borrow them for a while. See, we need to decorate a tree for a party . . . I mean, pageant . . . we're putting on tonight. Those ornaments would be perfect. I promise we'll bring them right back."

"A pageant, eh?" said Mr. Radford. "Is it a good one?"

"Um, sure," I said. "It's going to be great."

"Well then, be my guest," he said. "I'm happy to help out a fellow thespian."

"Fellow what?" I said.

"Thespian," he repeated. "You know—actor. I was something of an old hand on the stage myself as a young man. Why, my Hamlet is famous throughout Eerie."

He jumped up on the counter and began to recite. "To be or not to be," he shouted, holding out one hand. "That is the question."

He looked down at me. "Stirring, isn't it?"

"It's something else, all right," I said. "Very, uh, hammy, or hamlet-y, or something like that."

He jumped down again. "Wait until you see my Ophelia," he said.

"I'm kind of in a hurry," I said. "Maybe another time?"

"Certainly. Certainly."

I went and got the box. Then I went to join Simon outside.

"Thanks a lot, Mr. Radford," I called out as I left, but he was too busy to hear me. He was running around the store holding a broomstick between his legs and waving a candy cane around in the air.

"A horse! A horse!" he shouted. "My kingdom for a horse!"

"Did you get the ornaments?" Simon asked when I came out.

I held up the box. "Right here."

"Mr. Radford just let you have them?"

I looked back toward the store. "He was too busy

103

horsing around to really notice," I said. "Let's go, before we run into Mrs. Marlowe."

We walked back to Prudence Lively's house, taking turns dragging the tree and carrying the box. Luckily the snow was soft, and the branches didn't get broken at all on the way, even though we had to drag it over some pretty big drifts.

When we rang the bell, Lucy opened the door quickly. "Come in," she said.

We dragged the tree up the steps and into the house. Some snow came with it, and soon there were little drops of water on the floor as it melted.

"I'm glad you're here," she said. "There's so much to do."

"Who are you talking to, Lucy?" Prudence's voice floated in from the other room. A moment later, she came into the hallway. She was holding a holly wreath in her hand.

"These are the boys I told you about," Lucy said. "They're from town. I hired them to help us with the party tonight."

Prudence smiled. "Hello," she said, holding out her hand. "It's so nice to meet you. My name is Prudence Lively." She didn't recognize me as the boy who had delivered her package the day before.

"I'm Marshall," I said. "And this is my friend Simon."

Prudence smiled at Simon. "I'm so pleased that you

can help us out today," she said. "There's so much to do before tonight."

"I'm sure it will be a wonderful party," I said.

"I hope so," Prudence said. "I just adore Christmas Eve. I think I like it even more than Christmas. The expectation of what's to come is so thrilling, don't you think?"

"Oh, yes," I said. I was trying not to think about Prudence receiving the news that Henry was dead.

"We should get started," Lucy said, saving me from having to say anything at all.

"I'll leave you to it, then," said Prudence.

She left, and we got to work. First Simon and I took the tree into the big parlor. There was a tree stand in one corner, and we quickly put the tree into it and set it up. It was so tall that it nearly touched the ceiling.

"I hope we have enough ornaments to cover it," I said jokingly.

Lucy had some pine garlands, which she showed us how to wrap around the banister of the stairway. Then she stuck some pinecones into the swirls made by the branches and tied red velvet bows on the stair rails. When we were done, it looked great.

All morning we worked getting the house ready. We swept and dusted the floors and washed all of the big windows until they sparkled like diamonds. We put dozens of candles all over the house, and polished the big silver punch bowl until it shone like a mirror. Each time

I passed the painting of Henry Collins, I crossed my fingers and made a wish that everything would work out okay.

By noon we had most of the house ready for the party. I couldn't believe that Lucy usually did it all by herself. My arms ached from carrying tablecloths and scrubbing floors, and all I wanted to do was sit down and take a break. But there was still more to do.

"The tree has to be decorated now," said Lucy. "It's the last thing."

The three of us went into the parlor and got to work. I opened the box of ornaments and unwrapped the glass balls and fruit-shaped ornaments, the real glass icicles and angels with shiny gold wings. Each one went onto the tree.

"It's too bad you didn't have electric Christmas tree lights in nineteen-seventeen," I said. "They'd look pretty on the tree."

"Maybe these will look just as nice," said Lucy, opening the last box.

Inside were tiny candles. Each one was fitted into a little candleholder with a clip on the end. Lucy picked up one of the candles and fastened it to the end of a branch, where it stood up nice and straight.

We put the rest of the candles all over the tree, until it was covered with them. Then we stepped back to look at it.

"This will be amazing when they're all lit up," I said.

"Let's hope we get to that point," said Lucy. "Usually Miss Lively comes in here and knocks the tree over during her rage. Almost all of the ornaments are broken except for the few I manage to save."

"Those must be the ones we found in the box at World of Stuff," I said. "They must have been the only ones to survive."

As we were admiring our work on the tree, there was a knock on the door.

"Oh, no," I said. "It's the delivery man with the package. We forgot all about him. We have to get the snow globe before Prudence sees it."

All three of us turned at once and started to run for the door. But before we could even get out of the room, we heard Prudence's footsteps as she went to the door.

"Don't bother, Lucy," she called out brightly. "I'll get it."

"We're too late!" Lucy said.

Prudence had already reached the door and opened it. We stood in the hallway, watching as she took the package from the delivery man. Then she shut the door and looked at the address.

"It's from Henry!" she cried. "Lucy, it's a package from Henry."

We all watched as Prudence tried to remove the tape with trembling fingers.

"Oh, Lucy," she said. "Get me the letter opener. I'm shaking so much I can't get this tape off."

Lucy fetched the letter opener and handed it to Prudence, who quickly cut the tape and pulled it off the box. The she removed the letter and opened it. We all stared at her as she read.

"It's a present," Prudence said happily. "A Christmas present. How wonderful."

She opened the box and pulled out the snow globe. Lucy looked over at Simon and me. I hadn't wanted Prudence to receive the snow globe at all. I figured if she didn't have it, she couldn't use it to make her wish. But it was too late now. She had unwrapped it and was staring at it in wonder.

"Look," she said, shaking it. "It looks just like this house. I've never seen anything like it. And look how it snows when I shake it. It's as if someone captured a blizzard inside this ball."

She held it up for all of us to see.

"It's just beautiful," I said.

"Yes," said Lucy. "It's wonderful."

Prudence kept shaking the snow globe and laughing. "Wait until all of my guests see this tonight," she said. "None of them will believe their eyes."

She gathered up the letter from Henry and took it and the snow globe upstairs to her room.

"Now what are we going to do?" said Lucy, picking up the scattered pieces of tape and wrapping.

"It's not too late," I said. "We just have to make sure she doesn't get the message about Henry. And we have to make sure that the party goes on exactly as planned. We can't let anything upset her, or it will all be over. Remember, the soldier arrives shortly after the package."

"How will we get rid of him?" asked Simon. "We can't just tell him that no one is home. He'll wait. Or he'll come back."

I thought for a minute. "We won't get rid of him," I said. "Prudence will talk to him."

"What!" said Lucy and Simon. "We can't let her talk to him."

"Wait a minute," I said. "You haven't heard the rest. See, it won't really be Prudence he's talking to."

"What do you mean?" said Lucy.

"He'll be talking to you," I said, "only he'll think he's talking to Prudence Lively. I'll answer the door and pretend to be the butler. Then I'll call for you, and you'll pretend to be Prudence."

"I don't know if I can do that," Lucy said. "I'm not very good at pretending."

"It'll be easy," I said. "All you have to do is take the letter."

"But you don't look like a butler," said Simon.

I looked down at my clothes. He was right. I was covered in dust, and looked more like a chimney sweep than a butler.

"I think I have a coat you can put on," said Lucy. "Let me check."

She went into the kitchen and came back a minute later carrying a black coat.

"This belonged to the old butler," she said. "He left before I came, but some of his clothes are still here. I never got around to throwing them out."

I put the coat on. It was a little too big for me, but once I rolled the sleeves up and buttoned the front closed to hide my shirt, it looked okay. It was enough to fool anyone who didn't look too closely, anyway.

"That will have to do," said Lucy as she straightened my collar.

There was a knock on the door.

"That's him," I said. "Now, Lucy, you go in the other room. When it's time, you come out and pretend to be Prudence."

"I'm so nervous," Lucy said. "I can feel my hands shaking."

"That's okay," I said. "Just stay calm. This is important. Do it for Prudence."

Lucy and Simon went into the parlor. I took a few deep breaths and then went to the door and opened it. Standing on the step was the soldier I'd seen the day before.

"Good afternoon," he said. "Is this the home of a Miss Prudence Lively?"

"It is," I said in my best butler voice. "How may I help you?"

"I need to speak to Miss Lively," the soldier said. "It's official business. Is she home?"

As if on cue, Lucy came out of the parlor. She had removed her maid's cap and her apron, and she looked just like any other young woman.

"Who is it, Marshall?" she said.

"It's a soldier, ma'am," I said. "He wishes to speak with you."

Lucy came to the door. "Good afternoon," she said to the soldier.

The soldier removed his hat and nodded at Lucy. "Are you Miss Prudence Lively?" he asked.

Lucy looked quickly at me. "Yes," she said. "I am Miss Lively." She was doing well, and I hoped she could hold up.

The soldier looked uncomfortable. "I'm very sorry to tell you this," he said. "I have some bad news about a Mr. Henry Collins."

"Henry?" said Lucy, her voice filled with concern. "Is he all right?"

"I'm afraid that Mr. Collins is dead, ma'am," said the soldier. "He was killed in combat."

Lucy brought her hand to her face. She was holding a handkerchief in her fingers. When she pulled it away again, there were tears running down her cheeks.

"I'm very sorry to have to tell you this," the soldier said when he saw that she was crying. "I know it must be a shock."

He reached into his pocket and pulled out the familiar brown envelope. He handed it to Lucy.

"This is the official letter," the soldier said. "It contains all the information you need."

"Thank you," Lucy said softly. "Thank you for telling me."

The soldier nodded his head, put his hat back on, and

walked down the steps. Lucy came back inside and shut the door.

"Am I glad that's over," she said. "I've never been so nervous in my whole life. I was sure he was going to figure out that I wasn't Prudence."

"You were amazing," I said. "How did you make yourself cry like that?"

Lucy unrolled the handkerchief and showed it to me. Sitting in the middle of her palm was a big chunk of raw onion.

"I took it from the kitchen," she said. "When I held it up to my eyes, it made them tear up and made my nose run so I sounded like I was sniffling."

"That was a brilliant idea," I said. "It was really convincing."

"Now what do we do with the letter?" asked Simon.

"We hide it," I said. "Prudence can't see it until after the party."

"I feel awful hiding it from her," said Lucy.

"We have to," I said. "Otherwise she's going to curse herself—and us—to an even worse fate. Would Henry have wanted that?"

"No," said Lucy. "He would have wanted her to be happy."

"Is there somewhere you can put this where she won't find it?" I said.

"I'll put it in my dresser drawer," said Lucy. "Then

tomorrow, if everything works out, I'll say that it was delivered while she was out.''

''Good idea,'' I said. ''Now you'd better put your cap and apron back on before she sees you. We don't want to give her any reason at all to be suspicious.'' I handed her the butler's coat.

Lucy went and put the letter and coat away. When she came back, she was dressed in her usual outfit. And she was just in time. No sooner had she come back into the hallway than Prudence appeared at the top of the steps. She was dressed as though she were going outside.

''Lucy,'' she said as she came down the stairs. ''I think I'll go to the Christmas pageant in town this evening. It will relax me before the party begins. Besides, I like to see so many people in a Christmas mood.''

''That sounds like a marvelous idea, Miss Lively,'' said Lucy.

''Will you and the boys be able to get everything done on your own?''

''I think so,'' said Lucy. ''The food is almost prepared, and the boys have done a wonderful job getting the house ready.''

Miss Lively smiled. ''I'm so glad,'' she said. ''I'm so looking forward to this evening.''

She looked at the painting of Henry on the landing. ''I only wish Henry could see how beautiful everything looks.''

"I'm sure he's here in spirit," I said.

Prudence took her coat from the rack near the door and put it on. She put on a hat as well, and then some long gloves trimmed with rabbit fur.

"Oh, Lucy," she said. "I almost forgot. I'd like to place the snow globe in a place of honor this evening. I want everyone to be able to see it. Would you make sure you take it from my room and put it in a place of prominence?"

"Of course," said Lucy. "I'll put it right on the mantel in the parlor. That way it will catch the light from the tree."

"That would be perfect," said Prudence. "Now, I'll be back by seven-thirty. Guests aren't due until eight, so that should be plenty of time."

"Have a nice time," I said as Prudence left.

"Yeah," said Simon. "Enjoy the show."

As soon as Prudence was gone, Lucy shut the door and sighed.

"It's almost over," she said. "All we have to do now is make sure the party goes off smoothly."

"What could happen now?" said Simon. "We serve some punch, play some music, and it's all over."

"We need to find you something to wear," said Lucy, looking at our jeans and sneakers. "You can't come to the party looking like that."

"Where are we going to find clothes?" I said. "I

mean, I have a suit that my mother bought for me to wear to a funeral once, but that's it.''

Lucy thought. "In the attic," she said. "I know there are some boxes of old clothes that belonged to Miss Lively's brothers. I believe they just might fit you.''

We went upstairs, past the third floor, and into the attic. It was cold and drafty up there, and it looked as though no one had been there for years.

"Just how long have these clothes been in here?'' I asked Lucy as she rummaged around in a trunk at one end of the room.

"Not that long," she said. "At least, not in our time. Miss Lively's brothers are about your ages. They were recently sent off to boarding schools in the country, and their clothes were stored here.''

She lifted a black suit out of the box and handed it to me. "This one is for you," she said. "It belonged to Thomas.''

She pulled out another suit and handed it to Simon. "And this one was Andrew's,'' she said.

"I don't know if I can wear dead people's clothes,'' said Simon. "I feel sort of creepy.''

Lucy laughed. "They weren't dead when all of this happened,'' she said.

We went back downstairs and Simon and I changed in the spare bedroom we'd hidden in the day before. It felt really weird getting dressed up for a Christmas party that was being held by . . . Well, I wasn't exactly sure *what* Lucy and Prudence were. They weren't ghosts, exactly. They were just sort of caught in time. Anyway, I tried not to think about it as I put on the white shirt Lucy had also given me and tied the shiny black shoes she'd found wrapped in tissue paper.

When we were ready, we went out into the hallway, where Lucy was waiting. When she saw us, she clapped her hands.

"You look very handsome," she said. "Just like two gentlemen. You'll fit in perfectly."

"But how do we put these ties on?" said Simon, holding up the bow tie that went with the suit.

"I'll help you," said Lucy. She put the tie around Simon's neck and tied it quickly. Then she did mine.

"There," she said, stepping back. "You're all set. Miss Lively should be home shortly, and everything can start. All we have to do is light the candles on the tree and put the finishing touches on the food."

We started to go downstairs to finish getting ready, but halfway down, Lucy stopped. "I almost forgot," she said. "We need to get the snow globe."

"I'll get it," said Simon. "I remember where her room is."

He ran back upstairs while Lucy and I went down into the hall. He appeared above us a minute later, holding the snow globe in his hands.

"Got it," he said, and started down the stairs.

He was almost to the landing when he fell. His shoe

slipped on the carpet, and he lost his balance. Lucy and I watched in horror as he teetered on the edge of the steps, his hands moving back and forth as he tried to steady himself.

It was as though everything were happening in slow motion. Simon fell backward, his feet flying out from underneath him. The snow globe rolled out of his hands and bounced down the steps. It rolled across the landing, where it seemed to hang forever, balancing right on the very edge.

Then, as we all watched, it fell over the side and dropped onto the hallway floor below. There was a terrible crash, as it exploded into hundreds of pieces. The water ran out, carrying with it the little pieces of snow, which puddled around our feet like melted snowballs.

"**P**lease tell me it didn't break," said Simon. "Please tell me that you caught it."

"I didn't catch it," I said glumly.

Simon crawled over to the edge of the landing and looked through the rails. When he saw the mess on the floor, he let out a loud groan.

"Oh, no," he said. "I've ruined everything."

"What are we going to do now?" wailed Lucy. "If Miss Lively comes home and finds out that the snow globe has been broken, she's going to be heartbroken. She'll be sure to cancel the party."

"And if she doesn't have the snow globe to make a wish on, then we're in even bigger trouble," I said. "Because then tomorrow will come like it's supposed to, but we'll still be in the in-between time. Who knows what will happen then? We could all be stuck in nineteen seventeen, or you could be stuck in Eerie."

"Neither one of those things would be good," said Lucy.

"It's all my fault," said Simon. "I wish we could run out and buy another snow globe to replace it, like we did when I broke my mom's lamp playing ball in the house."

"But that globe was one of a kind," said Lucy. "There's no way to get another one."

I looked at the broken pieces of the globe on the floor. "Wait a minute," I said. "We *can* buy another one. We already have."

"What do you mean?" said Lucy.

"I already bought that snow globe," I said. "For my mother for Christmas. That's how all of this started, remember?"

"But if it's broken in my time, how will it still be whole in your time?" said Lucy.

"I don't know," I said. "All of this time stuff seems to be mixed up anyway. I don't think the rules apply here. But we don't have much time left. Prudence will be back in ten minutes, and then the guests will be here. It will take me at least twenty minutes to get to my house and back again." I pulled my coat on over my suit. "You two stay here and clean this up. I'll go get the snow globe. I'll be back as soon as I can."

I opened the front door and ran out into the winter night. My shoes sank into the snow, and it was hard to run, but I kept going as fast as I could. I had to get the snow globe and make it back to the house in time for the party.

By the time I reached my street, I was panting like crazy. The bow tie made it hard to breathe, and my feet were slipping on the ice-covered street. I checked my watch. I had already been gone almost twelve minutes. I hoped Simon and Lucy could distract Prudence long enough so that she wouldn't notice the missing snow globe.

I opened the door to my house and looked in. If anyone saw me in the suit, I was going to have a lot of explaining to do, and I didn't feel up to making up a good excuse. Luckily for me, my parents were in the living room, where I could hear them talking to each another.

"I wonder where Marshall is," my mother was saying. "It's not like him to miss trimming the tree on Christmas Eve."

"Oh, he and Simon are probably out sledding or something," said my father. "He'll be back soon."

If my plan didn't work, I was in big trouble. I ran past the living room and up the stairs to my bedroom. The snow globe was sitting safe and sound on my desk, right where I'd left it. I snatched it up, stuck it in my coat pocket, and went back downstairs. I ran out the front door before anyone could see me.

Running back to Prudence's house, I felt as though I was moving in slow motion. The snow fell gently around me as I pumped my arms and legs, trying to get them to move faster. It seemed to take hours to get back. But when I checked my watch again, I saw that it had only been twenty-five minutes since I left.

The first guests were walking up the steps as I arrived. Lucy was letting them in. I ducked past her and into the parlor, where Simon was busy stirring the punch in the big silver bowl.

"Where have you been?" he said. "We've been keeping Prudence out of here, but we can't stall her any longer. Did you get it?"

"Sure did," I said, taking the snow globe out of my pocket. I went over to the mantel and put it right in the center.

Just as I took my hand away, Prudence walked in.

"Oh," she exclaimed. "Everything looks so beautiful. The tree is exquisite."

Prudence herself was dressed in a beautiful dress made of scarlet velvet. It swept across the floor as she walked over to the mantel and gazed at the snow globe. She ran her fingers over it and sighed. Then she turned to me.

"Thank you for helping Lucy today," she said. "You boys have made this night unforgettable."

"Well, I know we'll never forget it," I said.

Prudence's guests were coming in now, and she went to greet them. I had no idea who any of the people were, or where they were coming from, but they definitely weren't from Eerie. Like Prudence, they were all dressed in old-fashioned clothes. The men wore tuxedos with white jackets, and the women were all wearing beautiful dresses. I felt like I was watching a play that took place in nineteen seventeen.

Only it was real. Simon was pouring real punch into real glass cups. Lucy was carrying a real silver tray with real sugar cookies on it. The heat coming from the fire in the fireplace was warm against my legs, and the voices of the women and men filling up the parlor were as real as mine.

"Can I have your attention," said Prudence. She was standing in the middle of the room holding what looked like a long silver wand in her hand. "It's time for us to light the candles on the tree. Since this year many of our loved ones cannot be with us because they are off fighting the war in Europe, I ask each of you to light a candle in memory of someone you love."

She went to the fireplace and stuck the end of the silver wand into the flame. The end caught fire, and I realized that it was a kind of lighter for reaching the candles that sat on the Christmas tree's branches. Prudence handed the lighter to a woman standing near her. The woman went to the tree and held the lighter to the wick of a candle. There was a flash of flame as it caught fire, and then the candle burned brightly.

The woman handed the lighter to the next person, who also lit a candle. The wand passed from hand to hand as each person in the room went to the tree and lit another candle, until soon the tree was burning with dozens of tiny flames. Then Prudence took the lighter again and went to the tree. Reaching up, she lit the final candle.

Lucy turned down the gas lights in the room until it was lit entirely by the candles on the tree. The flames flickered over the faces of the guests, and everyone watched silently for a few moments. Then Lucy turned the lights back up, and people started to talk. Lucy went into the kitchen and returned with trays of food, and the party got started.

For the next few hours, we were busy carrying food in and out of the parlor and making sure that everyone's punch glass was kept filled. Then someone put a record on the phonograph, and some of the people danced. From time to time I caught a glimpse of Prudence. She looked like she was having a good time. Then, before I knew it, it was after eleven, and people began to leave.

"Wait a minute," said Simon as the first people said their good-byes to Prudence and went to get their coats. "Is that it?"

"It can't be," I said. "Nothing really happened. We just had cookies and punch and a little dancing. That can't be all there is to this."

But there was nothing I could do to stop the people from leaving. One after the other they filed out the door, each one telling Prudence and Lucy what a wonderful party it had been and wishing them a merry Christmas. Soon we were the only ones left.

"We'll help you clean up," I said to Lucy. I wanted a chance to talk to her alone.

"Do you think we did it?" she said as soon as we were all back in the kitchen, away from Prudence.

"I really don't know," I said. "Nothing really feels different."

"I can't help but think we missed something," said Lucy.

From out in the other room we heard the sounds of crying. It was Prudence.

"Oh, no," I said. "She couldn't have found the letter."

The three of us ran into the parlor to see what had happened. Prudence was standing in front of the fireplace, looking at the snow globe. Tears were streaming down her face.

"Are you all right, Miss Lively?" I said gently.

She turned toward me and smiled a little. "I'm just sad," she said. "I wish more than anything that Henry were here with me. I don't know why, but I have this feeling that I won't see him again."

Lucy, Simon, and I exchanged glances.

"I know he would have wanted to be here tonight," I said. I couldn't think of anything else to say.

Prudence wiped her eyes. "I wish we could have just one dance together," she said. "Just one Christmas Eve dance."

I didn't know if I could end Prudence Lively's curse,

but I knew I could at least try to give her the one thing she wished for. I went over to the phonograph and turned it on. Then I put the needle onto the record, and the room was filled with music. I walked over to Prudence and held out my hand.

"Would you dance with me?" I asked her.

She looked at me, her eyes filled with tears. Then she took my hand. I put my other hand on her waist.

"I'm not a very good dancer," I said. "I'm sorry." I really had no idea what I was doing, but it felt right.

She didn't say anything as we started to dance. We moved around the room, lit only by the candles on the Christmas tree. Everything was bathed in a soft yellow glow. I didn't know what I was doing, but my feet seemed to move all on their own.

"This is our favorite song," Prudence said as we danced. "It's the first song we ever danced to."

She closed her eyes and started to hum along with the record. Over her shoulder, I could see Lucy and Simon watching us. And I saw something else. Something so strange I almost couldn't believe it.

On the landing, the painting of Henry Collins was glowing with a yellow light, just like the light from the Christmas tree. All I could do was stare at it in disbelief as the outline of Henry's figure burned brighter and brighter. Then he stepped out of the picture frame—just put one foot down on the carpet and followed it with the other, like he was walking through a door.

Henry Collins, still dressed in his soldier uniform, walked down the stairs and through the front hall. When he reached the parlor, he paused for a moment. Seeing him, Lucy and Simon gave soundless exclamations of surprise, watching with wide eyes as Henry walked into the room and came up to Prudence and me.

"May I cut in?" he said to me. His eyes were sparkling, and his voice was low and pleasant.

"Henry," said Prudence, "you came back."

"Yes," he said. "I came back for you. Everything is all right now. Did you think I'd miss dancing with you on Christmas Eve?"

I stepped away from Prudence, and Henry took her into his arms, holding her close. As the music played, they continued to circle the room. I stood with Lucy and Simon, watching.

"What's happening?" said Simon.

"I don't know," I said.

"It's true love," said Lucy. "As I said—true love never dies."

All of a sudden, the clock in the hallway began to chime midnight.

"It's Christmas morning," said Lucy. "We've done it. We've broken the spell."

As soon as she said that, the room began to change. The colors began to run together, like someone had spilled a glass of water over a watercolor painting. Henry and Prudence continued to dance, but they became dimmer and dimmer, until I could see the Christmas tree burning behind them.

All around us, the house was disappearing with each stroke of the clock. The walls were simply melting away. By the time the clock sounded for the eleventh time, Lucy, too, began to fade, like someone disappearing into the mist. She held up her hand.

"Good-bye," she said as the clock chimed for the twelfth time, her voice sounding like a thin gust of wind just before she went out of sight. "And thank you."

EPILOGUE

*S*imon and I were standing in the middle of what was left of a garden. It was covered in snow, and here and there the frozen remains of flowers stuck up out of the ground. There was no sign that Prudence's house had ever been there.

"Hey," said Simon. "We're wearing our own clothes."

The suits we'd been dressed in had gone, and we had on the same coats we'd put on when we left our houses that morning. I looked at my watch. It was one minute after midnight. The date spot on my watch face showed the numbers: 25.

"Lucy was right," I said. "We did it. It's Christmas."

"Where do you think they went?" asked Simon.

"I don't know," I said. "But wherever they are, I think they're happy."

That's when I noticed the snow globe. It was sitting

at my feet in the snow, half buried in the drifting whiteness. I picked it up and dusted the snow away from the glass. It wasn't broken at all.

Inside the globe, the snowstorm had stopped raging. I peered inside and looked at Prudence's house. The carolers still stood outside, their mouths open in song. Only now Prudence wasn't hiding behind the curtains. She was standing in the doorway. And standing next to her was Henry. He was wearing his uniform, and he had his arm around Prudence. Finally they were together forever.

"I guess this adventure is over," I said to Simon.

We walked home through the falling snow, not saying anything. All around us, all of Eerie slept silently, dreaming of Christmas morning. Only we knew that the whole town had been dreaming for three days.

"What are you going to do with the globe?" Simon asked me when we reached our houses.

"I think I'll keep it in the Evidence Locker in the Secret Spot," I said. "I think it's fine, but you never know when it might decide to act up again."

"But now you don't have a present for your mom," he said.

"Don't worry," I said. "I'll just give her the same gloves I gave her last year. She's never even taken them out of the box."

Simon laughed. "I guess I'll see you tomorrow, then. Merry Christmas, Mars."

"No," I said, waving good-bye. "Eerie Christmas. Eerie Christmas to all, and to all a good night."

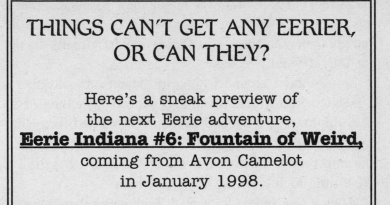

THINGS CAN'T GET ANY EERIER, OR CAN THEY?

Here's a sneak preview of
the next Eerie adventure,
Eerie Indiana #6: Fountain of Weird,
coming from Avon Camelot
in January 1998.

*O*utside, the morning had an icy chill and wind whipped up trash in the street. Weird. It should've been hot and muggy, like a normal summer day. Then I caught myself. Normal? Ha! Nothing is normal in Eerie, Indiana.

We jumped on our bikes and took a shortcut through downtown to the landfill. Mr. Periwig was taping a sign to the window of his barber shop.

WEDNESDAY: HAIRCUTS HALF PRICE.

BRING YOUR OWN BOWL.

I considered it. My hair had been getting a bit shaggy lately.

Eerie's landfill was the perfect spot for the annual

swap meet. The crater was larger than Kratatau. That's east of Java. Anything that couldn't be sold would be buried under a ton of dirt. Since it was already in the landfill, it would be easy.

Simon and I zipped by the traffic on our way there. I pedaled into a cold wind and sucked in a lungful of freezing air. For a second I thought I smelled formaldehyde, an odor I recognized from science class. I filed the information in my brain under "weird." Maybe I'd have time to investigate the smell later.

After a few miles the asphalt highway gave way to a rutted dirt road. Secretly I hoped to discover our missing walkie-talkies at the swap meet in someone's junk. Things have a way of turning up in unexpected placed here in Eerie.

Soon the dirt road was jammed with station wagons, minivans, and a school bus filled with retirees from the senior center. Horns honked and tempers flared as vehicles tried to inch their way to the dump, everyone wanting first dibs on the junk.

Simon and I stopped at the top of the landfill to catch our breath. An old lady sped by us on a unicycle. "Go for the burn!" she cried, her words riding the dust kicked up from her tire.

We looked at the landfill. It was a huge crater and there were rows of booths set up inside it. The booths were surrounded by twisted car frames and piles of disposable diapers that had been lying out there for years.

Off to one side, the entertainment was rehearsing. A band from the Texas Mosquito Festival was tuning up.

There was also a cluster of circus acts waiting to perform in the center of the landfill. A slender woman from the circus slipped a banner over her shoulders. It read CAUTION: WIDE LOAD.

"The circus must not be doing so hot these days," said Simon. "The fat lady couldn't weigh more than 99 pounds."

We pushed off down the steep road that eventually wound around to the landfill.

When my dad and I had been here earlier I'd picked a spot as far away as possible from my parents' booth. It didn't seem right to be competing with them. Besides, I didn't want to be near my sister, who was dressed like a garbage can.

Simon was unloading his wagon when a friend from school strolled over.

"What're you guys selling?" Sara asked, a stack of dog-earred paperbacks in her arms.

I found myself staring at her backpack, wondering if a pair of walkie-talkies was inside. *Stop it!* I told myself. This was Sara I was thinking about, winner of the Battle-of-the-Books (B.O.B.) competition.

The entire Lee family were bookworms, especially Sara's mom, Mrs. Lee, who devoured cookbooks, recipe by recipe. She owned Eerie's bakery, Sweet Tooth.

Sara had inherited a taste for literature, reading everything from Laura Ingalls Wilder and Mary Wollstone-craft Shelley to Martha Stewart and Betty Crocker.

"Just a bunch of junk," I finally said. I didn't want her spending her money here. I knew she was trying to save for the B.O.B. finals next month in Washington, D.C.

Sara opened one of her paperbacks. "What's the difference between dandruff and nose hair?" she asked.

"Beats me," I said.

Simon thought for a moment. "Nothing," he said. "They're both gross."

"That's right Simon!" She beamed at him. "Have you read this book?"

Simon shrugged. "I don't think so."

Sara started picking through our junk.

I could tell there wasn't anything she really liked. She just wanted to hang out with Simon. She'd had a crush on him for a few weeks, although Simon would never admit it.

Finally Sara walked toward the food booth run by Sir Lancelot. All the sausages you could spear for $2.95.

"See ya later," she said.

I nudged Simon. "Loved is like the common cold. You never know when you're going to catch it."

Simon blushed, his freckles matching his hair. "Not if I live a thousand years!"

Sara Lee's mom, I noticed, shared a booth with Harriet Nelson. They were selling baked goods: fudge,

cakes, cookies shaped like rock stars. The Grateful Dead
were the most popular cookies because the whole band
was sprinkled with nuts.

So far the swap meet seemed normal enough—at least
by Eerie's standards. But I knew from experience to
expect the unexpected. Being prepared wasn't everything in Eerie. It was the *only* thing.

Looking back on the day's events, I realize I should
have paid more attention to certain clues. Namely, the
smell of formaldehyde. Still, how could I have known
a mad scientist was lurking in our midst?

THINGS CAN'T GET ANY EERIER ... OR CAN THEY?

Don't miss a single book!

#1: Return to Foreverware
by Mike Ford
79774-7/$.99 US/$.99 Can

#2: Bureau of Lost
by John Peel
79775-5/$3.99 US/$4.99 Can

#3: The Eerie Triangle
by Mike Ford
79776-3/$3.99 US/$4.99 Can

Coming Soon

#4: Simon and Marshall's Excellent Adventure
by John Peel
79777-1/$3.99 US/$4.99 Can

#5: Have Yourself an Eerie Little Christmas
by Mike Ford
79781-X/$3.99 US/$4.99 Can